CONCRETE FEVER

CONCRETE FEVER
a novel

Nathaniel Kressen

with illustrations by
Jessie T. Kressen

SECOND SKIN
Brooklyn, NY

Printed in the United States of America.

First edition, 2011.

ISBN-13: 978-0-9840-356-0-1

Cover Design by Jessie T. Kressen.
Chapter Illustrations © 2010 Jessie T. Kressen.

Second Skin
secondskinbooks.wordpress.com

For Jessie.

"Be true like ice, like fire."
- *My father, quoting Bob Dylan.*

By the time winter hit, I had money from the inheritance and a bachelor pad on the Upper West Side. My father always said, Own, don't rent. Here was the living proof. He was gone and I was enjoying his old digs. It was a rich man's apartment in a rich man's neighborhood and I did my best to lower the standards. Despite all efforts I could do no wrong. When I cursed out a neighbor it was my grief talking. When I came home drunk it was a cry for help. I smoked indoors. I spat on the mailboxes. I dropped bottles out the window. I waited for the fallout.

At St. Bart's Catholic School I became one of those Treat with Caution kids. Got away with murder. Tested every patience protocol the administration frantically erected. Liked to drag others down with me and witness their consequences as opposed to my own. After each and every crime they offered me amnesty, and sure enough come the new year I had a 4.0 grade point average without turning in a single assignment. By January the back stairwell reeked of the joints I smoked before, during, between classes. Half the school's female population joined me there at some point. I used to have a nice girl. We dated for nearly two years. Dreamt up plans for college together followed by kids and white picket fences. Then I slept with her best friend. And after that the girl with dreads who she couldn't stand from homeroom. She had the guts to leave things when they stopped being good. I couldn't. I would have been happy being miserable. Since then I've admittedly gone a little girl-crazy. Sometimes I worried I might knock one of them up but you can't be too careful. A plane could hit your building any second and your only choice might be to jump.

After months of delay, my mind was made up. I grabbed a white shirt out of the dresser. Fumbled with the necktie but eventually got it right. I slid open the closet and thumbed through his old jackets, untouched going on five months. They looked like withered capitalist corpses, strung up one after the other. I chose one on the end. Simple, black, tailored. No idea if it would fit. I wanted it to hang loose, prove there was difference between the old man and myself. It shoved my arms drunkenly into the sleeves and pulled it over my shoulders. The damn thing fit like a glove. For a few minutes I fought gravity trying to pull on the matching slacks. To my delight, the waistband was loose. I pulled the worn belt from my jeans and looped it into the dry-cleaned suit bottoms, doubling an inch or two of fabric over itself. I took a sip of scotch, then another. I considered leaving a note but couldn't think of anything to write that wouldn't sound dishonest. I left the apartment before realizing I'd grabbed my keys out of habit. I stared at the closed door a minute, then entered the stairwell to head up to the roof.

I started walking ledges after the city's first frost. Made it more likely I'd slip and fall the twelve stories, end up a piece of modern art on display across Amsterdam Avenue. My father always said to follow in his footsteps. Capitalism makes the world run. Buy low, sell high type shit. Mind you, this fixation of his didn't mean he'd stop by the Brooklyn apartment any more than once every few months. He paid child support and private school tuition, so he considered himself a good parent. His connections got me accepted early decision to a top-tier business program with a focus on undergraduate economics. When the acceptance letter arrived he'd already been dead a few months. I decided to follow his footsteps another way. I convinced myself the monster inside me had to have come from somewhere and it must have been him. That he'd been like me and depended on something outside of himself to end a bad situation. That he hadn't been jumping to save himself at all.

Twelve stories up anything seems peaceful. The honking car horns become a symphony. The trees stretch up at you like a little kid's arms. You imagine falling would feel like floating. Everything seems peaceful twelve stories up, unless there's a stranger on your roof, on your ledge, blocking your way the one night you've worked up the drunken courage to go through with it.

I pulled her back and pinned her down before I even realized I was moving. The night spun around me and I lost the music in my head. All I could think of was the cold.

You mind if I got up? she asked.

I rolled over and let her sit up, adjust her colorful patched skirt and necklaces caught in her hair. I collected my breath to stomach the lump in my throat. I could only imagine how much worse scotch would taste coming up than going down. I was still a novice at anything past beer but I'd been making a strong show of it in recent months

3

with the help of my father's liquor cabinet. Hard to imagine how he'd held on to the number of bottles he did when I was able to breeze through them so easily.

Fingers snapped in front of my eyes. You there? I forced myself to look at her. I had the sinking feeling that my eyes were betraying something. She seemed to notice whatever it was because she stared at me in the quiet for what seemed like forever. For a moment I thought I blacked out but then I realized she'd laid her forehead against mine and was whispering consolations. The streetlight glimmered off what I could see of her necklaces. She exhaled softly, a cloud escaping past my chin. I leaned closer, smelling strawberries. Her mouth inches from mine.

Why are you jumping? I asked, throat closing over the last word. She didn't understand so I repeated the question. She fixed her eyes on me like I was about to pin her again.

What, like, *jump* jump? I was dancing.

On the edge of a roof?

Yeah...?

Odds are you fall.

Screw the odds.

I contracted my stomach muscles until my lungs emptied. I sat there clenched, shaking, wondering if the dull hot weight would feel the same if I were drowning. Finally an itch snuck into my chest and I coughed until I recovered.

She sat there all the while, watching impassively. I tried to catch her blinking but always seemed to be a moment too late. She asked if she could bum a cigarette. For some reason I told her I didn't smoke. She said that that was stupid and smoking rocked and rose to fetch her bag from the other side of the rooftop. She unzipped a case with a smiling monkey on it and pulled out a pack of rolling tobacco and papers. She returned almost at a skip and plopped back down on the roof next to me, cross-legged. Then she promptly began to roll the most lop-sided cigarette I ever saw in my life. I told her as much and she dared me to do better which I did, despite my fingers going numb from the cold air. She asked how and I told her I'd been smoking a lot of pot recently. She asked if I had any on me, but once again I lied and told her I didn't.

She blew a perfect smoke ring that broke apart on the wind. I wasn't going to fall, she added as though our debate had never stopped. I have impeccable balance. I have wings. I'm an angel.

I don't see any wings, I said.

They're under my clothes.

Show me.

It's cold.

Come on.

Nope.

Fine.

Pause. You should've asked me again.

Why?

Because if you ask me three times I have to show you.

Can I see them?

No.

But that was the third time.

It won't work now, I told you the secret.

Suddenly it crossed my mind that she might be my guardian angel but I didn't want to call attention to it. I told her I didn't believe her. She answered no problem. After all, it was my loss.

For the first time I noticed the garbage strewn about the rooftop. Smashed CDs, torn clothing, and remnants of things unrecognizable. I mentioned it and she smiled. Earlier that night she broke into her ex-boyfriend's apartment looking for a ring she'd given him. He caught her in the midst of it so she stuffed what she could into her bag and raced out the window, up the fire escape, and onto the roof. Then she ran from rooftop to rooftop until she ended up on mine where she smashed and tore his things until there was nothing left to do but dance.

After her story I offered her a drink from the flask in my pocket. I had found it in my father's cabinet downstairs, and even though it reeked of yuppie wealth I started carrying it around places. As far as I could tell it was pure silver and had a custom design imprinted (worth noting that my father wasn't always a capitalist drunk but at one point a promising young artist). She said the flask looked cheap. I nearly fell in love with her right there.

She gagged on the first taste and asked what I was drinking rubbing alcohol for. I told her it was an expensive brand of scotch and she rolled onto her back laughing. I gulped it down no problem. I suppose the proper etiquette would be to sip and savor the stuff but I was looking to keep my drunk going. I could only taste the burn at that point anyway. I took out my cigarettes and offered her one. It could have been my imagination or my drunken ego, but I swear her eyes flickered with attraction now that I was exposed a liar. Not a smoker, huh? She took two out of the pack, swept her hair back and stashed the extra one behind her ear. She leaned in for a light and I obliged. We smoked there in silence, the cold no longer bothering me.

Tell me something honest, she said at last. Something brutally honest. Tell me the one thing you'd never want anyone to know.

Why should I?

Because I asked you to. She took a sharp puff of the cigarette and exhaled just as swiftly. Come on, we're strangers, what does it matter? You like my company don't you?

Now this could be a trick, I remember thinking. I stepped back, which is to say I tried to jolt my brain into action before answering, and looked her over for what could have been the first time. Fierce eyes with an abundance of eyeliner. Little make-up otherwise. Red streaks in a tangle of dark hair, who knows if they were natural or not. Teeth poised to bite behind full cupid lips. A thin, wiry frame. A coat that could have cost two dollars or two hundred depending on where she bought it. Long necklaces, dangling earrings, tons of bracelets and rings. A patched skirt that reached below her knees. Sketchers. On some level I must have known that any time spent with her was going to mean playing by her rules, but hindsight is 20-20. At the time I thought my options were either her or the Amsterdam Avenue sidewalk.

Sure, I told her. I like your company.

So, keep the night going. If you tell me something really sick I'll stay. If not I'll go. Something really sick, okay? Go.

I have allergies.

Obviously not a fan of my humor. She pulled the top of her coat shut and reached for her bag. I didn't ask for a joke, I asked for an honest answer.

Hold on a second, what's your name? I was surprised by the desperation in my voice.

Why? She was standing now.

I stood in turn. Come on.

Nathaniel Kressen

If you can guess my name I'll stay. She looked ready to run to another rooftop.

I don't know... Gypsy.

That stopped her. She adopted a few poses where we stood, trying the name on. She lifted her eyes to me. Not bad, but I want an honest answer. Something brutally honest.

My drunk was steadily evaporating so maybe that's why my mind was elsewhere, but honestly that's no explanation for what came out of me. I returned her stare and found myself saying, When I came up here I was thinking of jumping.

Wind. Car horn. Imagine her expression. Why? she said at last.

Because life is a headache.

Is that all?

It would be stupid to ride it out for another fifty years if this is all there is to it.

That's when she named me Jumper. She said that way I'd keep being honest with her.

She grabbed the flask and drank. Smooth sailing this time, only a hint of disgust on her face. What made tonight so special? she asked.

No dinner plans.

So call someone up.

Right.

Why not? You're dressed for it.

I fingered my father's tie absently, loosening it from around my neck. Felt like my body temperature had risen a few degrees.

Why not? she repeated.

You're like a little kid with all these questions.

Don't you have anyone to call?

If I did, would I be up here?

Tough life you got.

I think so.

She took another drink and handed the flask back. I weighed it in my hands, she wasn't taking it slow. I'd go out to dinner with you if you paid me. I'd even act like I liked you.

Just then the moon came out full from behind a cloud. The shift in light made her look up. I feel like a jerk-off saying it but she really did look beautiful. The moonlight all around her and the symphony starting to register from below again. For a split second I felt whole.

When there's a full moon out, she said, I feel like magic can happen any second. I look up and pretend like everything bad in my life floats away and I'm left as pure as the moon. You ever feel like that?

She caught me staring. An idea formed in that half-crazed state of mine and it was all I could do to keep from jumping over the ledge and being done with it all. I'd drunk myself to a conclusion and wasn't ready to give it up so quick. This stranger, hot though she may be, was making me lose sight of how I sabotaged things with the only girl that got me and couldn't care less about it. How there'd been half a dozen since and none of them mattered. How it had been years since I felt anything except a nagging darkness. Common sense would say my depression was a form of grief but truthfully that wasn't it. My father couldn't have been a more heartless son of a bitch and it wasn't like he was a real part of my life. Truth was, this thing had always had a grip on me and his death was just an excuse to set it free. I didn't believe in the goodness of people, had had enough of playing pretend, and yet on the very night I decided call it quits, here was this gypsy chick talking magic in the moonlight. So for whatever reason, to prove myself right I guess, I decided to give the world one last shot.

Let's do it, I ventured. What you said.

What, dinner?

Sure, but – what if we made it a game? Act out a first date. Take it from there. Make up a second, third. We could play out a whole relationship, all tonight.

You want to do this why?

Like you have any other plans tonight aside from scaling buildings?

She turned to go but I grabbed her arm. Her expression told me I squeezed harder than intended but I was beyond caring.

You really think magic can happen, why don't you prove it? One night, that's all I'm asking. When it's over I'll pay you. We're strangers. What's it matter?

She pried her arm free but didn't back away. She was so close the steam from her breath hit me square in the face. I couldn't place the look in her eyes. You were really going to off yourself tonight? I nodded. She flicked away the last of her cigarette. How much you offering?

I reached into the jacket pocket opposite the flask and pulled out a thick billfold. Securing it was a gold money clip that probably cost hundreds in and of itself. I suspected a few of the larger bills would be enough to sell her on the idea. Instead I handed her the whole thing, clip included. I had more cash in my wallet, not to mention a debit card tied to a bloated bank account. In any case, I didn't have any long-term plans. Her eyes fixed on the money in her hands. She ran her fingers along the bills so their ends flipped softly against one another. I doubted it was her way of counting.

Just pure dumb shock. I asked her if we had a deal, and it seemed to break her from whatever thoughts she was having. She stuffed the cash down her shirtfront and said, Fuck yeah, we do.

I opened the door to the stairs and it creaked something awful. A nasty grease came off on my hand and I wiped it clean on the white wall of the stairwell.

Hot, she said.

Suddenly I missed the first step and landed with my foot inverted on the one below. Heat shot up the outside of my leg. I crouched against the stairs and grabbed for my ankle.

Aw. You're a lightweight!

You going to call me that all night?

What's your real name?

I don't like my real name.

I'm keeping the money if you bust yourself.

I sat on a stair and forced circles with my foot.

She knuckled a rhythm on the wall. Great first date.

I swallowed the surge of pain and stood. If I can make it to the elevator I'll be alright.

Oh joy. She coughed and skipped ahead and I did my best to keep up. The elevator opened. Which floor is yours?

I thought we were grabbing dinner.

Which one? she repeated.

It's this one, the penthouse.

She stepped in the elevator and said that's hot again over her shoulder. She pressed the buttons for every floor except mine and each time the door opened she spat into the hallway. This went on the full eleven floors.

Why? I asked at one point.

Why not? she shot back.

We stepped out into the cold. I know this ritzy bistro place we can go, I suggested.

You don't kid around, do you?

If we're doing this we're doing it right.

As long as you're not expecting me to drop my panties at the sight of a salad fork.

It rained earlier so the streets were warped with color in the way that makes first timers fall in love with the city. Streetlights transformed everything into old photographs. Traffic lamps cast shifting patterns on the pavement. Exaggerated shadows made even the most mundane couple look like they were out of a Fellini film. Everywhere and everyone, sexy as all hell. That's what I'd been told anyway. Born and raised in the city, I couldn't appreciate it. All I saw was the same old garbage.

I smiled at her, a sparkle in my eye, playing the role we set for ourselves. Girls don't think guys calculate those things but we do. It's four parts excitement, four mystery, two vulnerability. The recipe changes based on the relationship's timeline but that one works fine early on. That's what I threw her. She responded by stopping in her tracks. We'd better set some ground rules, she said.

I limped to a stop. What'd you have in mind?

That look of yours for starters.

What look? I asked innocently.

Don't play dumb. Stuff like that's off-limits. You launch into this like you're playing The Game, it's never going to work.

This is a game.

Not a game, she said pointedly. The Game. The one where your charm and disrespect are probably enough to get you laid.

I coughed to keep from laughing.

She smirked but didn't break. What's so funny?

Usually, if a girl is bold enough to call me on it, she's playing the same game I am.

Sigh. Here's the deal. Magic can happen within The Game. People can torture one another and end up finding something good in spite of themselves. But that takes time and reflection, neither of which we have tonight.

So what are you proposing?

I'm saying we be open to what happens if two people are actually honest.

Within the lie, I countered.

Her forehead wrinkled.

We're acting this thing out start to finish in one night, right? Not exactly realistic. And, devil's advocate, neither of us is going to legitimately open up tonight.

Then we might as well quit now, she said, walking away.

What did I say? I called after.

She spun to face me, already a good distance down the block. I waited but she just stood there silent, eying me.

I limped closer. Why are you leaving?

I thought we were on the same page.

And we're not?

She started rummaging in her bag. I caught a glimpse of the cash inside her bra as she bent over. Not looking at me, she said, It's going to be a waste of time if that's how you see it.

Is that right?

Seems like it.

Give me the money back then.

What's the point? she asked loudly. You're just going to jump off your roof tonight anyways.

A dozen pedestrians slowed mid-step. My face went hot. I lurched forward so I was nose to nose with Gypsy. She stayed her ground. Lifted her eyes. Her hair smelled sweet, a mixture of sweat and smoke. I lost my words. Tried to collect myself.

Meanwhile she started beaming, a crazed energy consuming on her face. Like a kid picturing the best way to break her new toy. She said, We can cause each other a lot of grief, can't we?

I forced my voice lower to seem more in control than I felt. Yeah, but in that good way.

Her reply came soft. I didn't say I wasn't going to do this. It's just going to be hard finding magic if we're stuck in the same old patterns.

Isn't that the point?

Maybe, she answered. Her breath showed in the air and floated past.

I noticed the crowd had split, apparently bored with no jumper in sight. It's part of it, I offered. You can't change the circumstances to affect the outcome.

So what are you thinking, rules-wise?

A cold wind picked up. I zipped my jacket up to the neck and dug my hands into my pockets. How about no real names, for starters. Just Gypsy –

- and Jumper, she chimed in.

Sure, I continued. No breaking character...

Where does the truth fit in?

I shrugged. We're not going to know the difference. Thing is though, we have to treat everything like it's real. So whatever you bring up, it had better be convincing.

14

CONCRETE FEVER

She smiled and reached for the cigarette behind her ear. The one she'd stolen off me earlier. I lit it for her and she inhaled greedily. So is that all? she asked, smoke spilling out with each word.

You think we need a safe word?

Where's the fun in that? she said.

I eyed her. Fine, no safe word. And no leaving until the game is through.

What decides that?

Fuck if I know. This is my first fake relationship.

She grinned. I doubt that's true.

Okay, my first overtly fake relationship. That more accurate?

Who knows, Jumper? If tonight goes south, it might be your last one too. With that she skipped a few paces ahead and stopped. You coming? I'm starving.

I led her a block west and two north to a French bistro my father introduced me to. I couldn't imagine a more suitable location to kick off the relationship to end all relationships. The menu was uninventive and overpriced. The décor tasteless rich. The wait staff intentionally rude. When we arrived the night was in full swing. The clientele was perfectly matched to the place. Well-groomed businessmen flaunting their paychecks to impress designer-clad ladies. There was a half hour wait but I slipped the maitre d' a few crisp bills and we were escorted directly to an open table. I took liberty ordering the wine.

Our conversation leaned toward the mundane at first. We found a rhythm knocking the bad classical music but soon fell back into silence. The food was solid but forgettable. Her enthusiasm from the sidewalk wilted before my eyes. Our game was less than an hour in and she was quickly losing interest. I did nothing to fix it. She excused herself after the entrees, ditching half the food on her plate.

I gave the bottle a shake and the final drops of wine slid into Gypsy's glass. She'd be back from the restroom any minute and I was playing the part of the gentleman. In the meantime I stole swigs from the flask. It caught the attention of a woman at another table. She was in her thirties, attempting to look younger but failing. I'd heard her snap at the waitress, complain to her friends, and now I was the object of her affection. I blew her a kiss. Her eyes widened. I loosened my tie. I undid a button. I licked the air. She crinkled her face, ordered the man across from her to get the check and stalked off to the bathroom. He glanced in my direction but I was focused on the dessert menu.

My father was into the finer things as he put it. During our rare visits he would try to groom me. Said that as long as I kept a well-stocked wine cellar I'd have enough sway to keep both my wife and mistress happy. That was when I was twelve. He introduced me to cubans the night of my thirteenth birthday. Learn to appreciate a good cigar and you'll make executive by the time you're thirty. I got so sick that night I missed the next day of school. Of course he dropped me back at the Brooklyn apartment and was unreachable by phone. My mother was out of commission following a night of Côtes du Rhône and Xanax. I think those hours on the bathroom floor might have been the last time I prayed. My entire body caving in. I could scarcely breathe. Kept repeating anyone stupid enough to smoke deserved that what they got, I'll never do it again, just get me through the night. I never knew if anyone was listening. Either way by fourteen I was smoking a pack and a half a day.

I took another swig and caught sight of Gypsy. She slapped a cell phone shut, her face heavy. With an audible sigh she fell into her chair, stuffed the phone in her bag and shot me a glowing smile. The transition was seamless, the private frustration nowhere to be found. I'd entered this game with a real actress.

Thought you'd fallen in, I said.

Just powdering my nose so I can look as beautiful as possible for you.

You didn't have to do that.

You've shown me a wonderful time tonight, she replied. Candlelit dinner, roses. Everything a girl could ask for on a first date.

I glanced at them, lying across her steak knife like blossoming corpses, bought on a whim from a vendor down the block. You like them?

They're my favorite.

Good.

She downed her wine and glanced around for the waitress. She thought we'd get busted when I ordered the first bottle. Lucky for us I had a face that read twenty-five and clothes that promised a worthwhile tip. You want to order another bottle? She eyed me greedily. I got the impression she drank whenever she got the chance and stomached however much she could. I found the waitress and gave a half-nod to the empty bottle. She took the hint and disappeared in the direction of the bar.

So your family's loaded, she remarked.

I considered how to answer - fact or fiction. They do alright for themselves.

You're being modest.

Maybe I'm embarrassed.

Nathaniel Kressen

She scoffed. What is there to be embarrassed about?

The flash, the glitz, it's not all it's cracked up to be. Sometimes I can't tell who likes me for me, and who pretends to like me for my money.

I can't imagine who would do such a thing, she said casually.

Happens every day, I answered, shaking my head.

... So I must be in line for some pretty nice gifts, huh?

I repressed a smile.

I can picture us now. Sailing the seven seas on your yacht, the wind in our face, your monkey butlers serving us banana daiquiris.

You're nuts, I said.

I have to be, otherwise you'd get bored.

No I wouldn't.

As if to prove me wrong, she clamped her mouth shut. The silence wore on, the sound of clinking silverware from nearby tables seeming louder with each passing second.

Finally she said, I like you in that suit.

Yeah?

It suits you well.

I grinned in spite of myself.

Don't worry, she continued. I won't tell anyone I saw you smile... Look at all the fashionable women who come here. They really know how to work an outfit. You'd never suspect how many of them were going on forty. If there's one thing science teaches us, it's that with enough money no one has to get any older. Ever... I, meanwhile, feel underdressed.

You look beautiful.

Not mesmerizing? she asked sharply.

Yes, mesmerizing, I said.

Not sexy?

Absolutely sexy.

Not fantastically gorgeous to the point of being deadly to anyone who lays eyes on me?

Sure, I said.

Can you give me a foot massage?

With that she kicked off her shoes and shoved one of her feet in my crotch. I hate to admit it but I caught myself checking to see if any neighbors noticed. After we leave, I said.

Who cares what people think?

Me.

That's disappointing.

I'm a disappointing guy.

Her foot disappeared and she slipped on her shoes. Why was I pissed at her? There was some threshold she'd crossed, but I had no idea it existed. It was like our game had become some boxing match to decide the bigger bad ass and I'd been knocked down in the first round.

Get the check, she said, I'm going to have a cigarette.

Wait and I'll have one with you.

I'll wait for you out front.

Just stay here.

I want a cigarette.

You'll have one in two minutes.

The waitress stood over us with the bottle of wine. Leave it corked, I said. We'll take it with us.

I'm sorry you can't do that, sir.

Look, I'll leave a good tip, just set it down and get us the check.

She looked offended but did it all the same. Gypsy sat on the edge of her seat with her coat on, glaring at me with eyes that made me want to run for my life and tear her clothes off simultaneously. I collected myself, took a breath and tried to start fresh.

It'll be good having the wine to walk with.

No response.

We just need to get a paper bag or something.

Still nothing.

So, we covered me, now I want to hear about you.

What do you want to know?

Did you grow up around here?

Don't be conventional. It's boring.

What do you want me to ask?

Something you actually want to know.

Breathe. Exhale. Don't choke her...

But first give me a sip from that flask you're hiding.

I motioned toward the table next to us but Gypsy held her hands out all the same. I pulled it from my lap and she snatched it from me, ran her fingertips over the imprint, considered my expression.

It takes a certain type of guy to carry comfort around in his pocket. Anytime you're uneasy and don't know what to say you just take a swig of this and things become a whole lot easier. You can tell me I'm sexy without your palms sweating.

The waitress returned and I gave her my card without looking at the check. Gypsy swigged before she left. When the waitress returned for my signature Gypsy drank again, longer this time, adding a glugging noise for effect. I realized she wasn't drinking at all, purely doing it to piss off the waitress. It worked. She snatched the signed receipt from us and stalked out of sight. By now we were drawing dirty looks from staff and clientele alike. I glanced at Gypsy, who was leaning so far forward it looked like she was going to fall out of her seat.

Tell me I'm sexy, she urged, not bothering to keep her voice down. And let me see your palms while you say it.

Reluctantly, I put my palms up, as if someone had a gun pointed at me. You're sexy, I muttered.

Say it like you want me.

I do, I said, forcing myself to play along.

More than anything?

More than anything.

Would you go to the ends of the earth for me? Do anything I asked of you? Jump off a roof if I asked you to?

I said yes. She said we might just be a match made in Heaven.

After a hurried exit, we headed back to my place for a corkscrew. There was admittedly some tension on the walk over, at least on my side, as to what that meant but we'd sworn no breaking character. If sex was in the cards so be it. One less illusion of magic, one step closer to the ledge.

We took the elevator up. No spitting this time?

Shoot I forgot! She pressed the remaining buttons and spat the rest of the way.

I'd brought a few girls home since I took over the place. Most were a combination of drunk and baked by the time we got there and let me guide the way. Not Gypsy. She bounded through the door the second the key turned and headed straight for the kitchen. She made a racket pulling the drawers open until she found what we'd come for. I put my keys down and slid an arm out of my coat.

What do you think you're doing? she called. You didn't expect me to spread my legs on a first date, did you? She skipped my way, then paused a moment at the floor-to-ceiling windows overlooking Verdi Square. Shitty view, she said. Before I could respond she whipped past me and was back on the elevator clucking for me to follow. She spat the whole way down.

It's so weird you have a doorman. I glanced back, we were still well within earshot. Do you like, tip him every time you go out to grab a bagel and lox?

I don't eat fish.

Lucky you. She paused at a parked SUV and pulled a Support Our Troops ribbon off its bumper. She slapped it on the next car up and kept walking. I asked her where we were going. She motioned to the sky and suggested we crack open the wine.

We walked west, passing the brown-bagged seventy dollar bottle of Languedoc between us. I was still limping but my ankle hurt less now that a second bottle was underway. Unlike scotch I had unfortunately developed an elitist palate for wine – score one for the old man – and it was nearly impossible for me to enjoy the parties thrown by my classmates. I'd been utterly disgusted with their selection of two buck chuck and boxed wine and ended up picking the locks to their parent's stores. I couldn't articulate it but there was some correlation between trust funds and the lack of creativity. We lived in New York and fake ID's were a dime a dozen. There was no excuse for scrounging. I still got invitations but rarely attended. To be honest it made me nauseous to have left the boroughs and taken up residence in their neighborhood.

We hit grass soon enough, passed underneath the highway and headed straight for the Hudson. When we got to the railing she swung herself up and sat with her legs dangling over the rocks. And that is how you follow the moon, she said as she grabbed for the bottle.

So basically you walk in one direction until you hit a river?

You're such a romantic. She swigged and wiped a few stray drops from her mouth with the back of her hand. I didn't think you were going to call me after the other night.

Huh?

Don't get me wrong, I had a good time. But that restaurant?

You mean...

Short skirts do not look good when you're sporting varicose veins, ladies. Get a mirror and dress your age, am I right? Don't worry though. I know it was probably first date jitters taking me there. That's why I'm glad you called. Tonight's date is going to go a whole lot better, I just know it.

I had to admit, the girl had skills.

We passed the bottle for a few minutes, just letting the quiet fall over us. The wine hit my stomach and my vision blurred. Nonetheless I was digging the spot she'd chosen. The lights on the water, the city behind us, no sound but the steady hum of traffic and the soft lapping of the tide. It was cold enough that no one else was around. I wondered if the open air had her waxing poetic in her head the same way I was. I stood taller and stayed quiet. The last thing I wanted to do was voice my thoughts out loud.

You see that tower down there? she asked, breaking the silence. There used to be an orphanage there, the state tore it down. I was lucky enough to get lost in the transition.

I cocked my head, staring at the condo development south of us. You're messing with me, right?

Stone cold stare.

Nathaniel Kressen

I turned for another look, still no reaction from her.
They wouldn't build an orphanage that close to the river.
Is your dad an architect or something?
It's common sense.
I don't know what to tell you, that's the spot in all its
glory.
Wind. Boat horn. Another look back. I tried getting
things on track. I like it on the river, you can barely hear the
traffic.
She sipped on the wine, then turned to me like she was
interested. It always makes me feel alone. Some parks just
creep me out, like no one can hear you scream type deal.
Riverside at least you know you're in civilization. When I
grow up I'm going to have a full-floor apartment overlooking
the Hudson. With monkey butlers and shit.
Again with the monkey butlers.
You can't deny you want one... Every so often I see kids
who were in the orphanage with me. You want to see all-
stars. Skin and bones starving, multiple arrests. That place
messed everyone up.
Everyone's got their baggage.
What's yours?
I tried to sound casual. Past relationships, family stuff,
the list goes on.
Let me guess. You're from a white-collar, suburban
family somewhere upstate with two cars in the driveway.
Only child but plenty of pets, spoiled rotten on the holidays.
You found your dad's liquor cabinet sooner than most but
you were still a long shot from being the bad boy in class.
You were the quiet one. You wrote poetry for the school
newspaper which led you to the big city where everyone has
their own private sob story they love to tell.

24

CONCRETE FEVER

My family, seriously, is enough to make you want to slit your wrists.

Spare me. The last thing I want to do is compare lists.

My next argument died in my throat. She was so off the mark it should have been entertaining. So why wasn't it?

I shouldn't have brought you here, she said.

Why?

Because we're comparing tragedies on a second date.

What, you mean your orphanage story?

We came here because I wanted to start off with something real.

Well that doesn't make a whole lot of sense now does it?

Back to silence.

I had that drunk where you only realize the anger in your voice after it's got out and in that state you're not sure you regret it. A moment later I realized I'd been staring at a passing boat with the intensity of a stalker. It slipped by slow-motion, nothing changing, nothing making much sense on shore. Out the corner of my eye I saw she'd climbed back over the railing and was doing something. Turned out she was trying to roll herself a cigarette. She'd been copping mine but I guess those were off-limits now. I offered to roll her a decent one but she cursed at me. I turned back to the water. If the game ended here it would make for a damn expensive couple of hours, I thought. But somehow I was relieved. She talked magic, I didn't believe her. I came in with nothing and was alright going out the same way. If the shore was a few stories taller I might have ended it right there. As it was I'd have to limp the avenues back to my apartment. I figured it might be worth it grabbing a cab.

I came here a lot when I was younger, she said out of nowhere. I'd spend hours looking out. One night, when there was no one around, I decided I'd swim to Jersey. I climbed the railing, lowered myself down and swam as far from the shore as I could. Soon I got so tired my entire body shut down. I yelled for help. I started to sink. And I realized, if no one was coming, it was up to me whether I lived or died. When I got back to the shore I felt this clarity I never felt before. But it faded after a few days, and then it disappeared altogether. I try connecting to people on that level but it never works. Something always holds them back.

Her cell phone rang. She glanced at the caller's name, pressed Ignore, and shoved it back into her bag. Then her eyes darted back out over the water.

CONCRETE FEVER

Nathaniel Kressen

Gypsy reminded me of someone but I couldn't place it. Out of the corner of my eye I took her in. Isolated her features. Tried to make the connection. Her hands, her profile. Did no good. I weighed her voice, her vocabulary. Temper. In the end I just retreated to the same tired thoughts about my ex. We'd had good times, tough times. I remembered every detail, just not my motivation for fucking her over. She'd been the first one to find me after the attacks. Stayed all night. Rode me till my head was empty. Held me when I cried, gave me space when I asked for it. But she never left. She trusted we'd make it through my father's death intact. My dick had other plans and executed them first chance it got. In the end, my only regret was that the girl I'd chosen to cheat on her with turned out to be a boring lay. Just laid back and took it, barely made a sound. I resented my girlfriend for upping my standards in that department. We'd never had problems connecting. Nevertheless, my self-hatred had me doubting. I kept screwing around and the rumors reached her. I didn't bother denying it. The damage was done. The goal had been met. I pushed away the best thing in my life for good.

Gypsy was not my ex. Far from it. Far as I could tell, where my ex showed compassion and tenderness, Gypsy offered impatience. She had no desire to be a shoulder to cry on. She wanted excitement. Breathing somewhat in unison with her, mindlessly staring out over the Hudson, I realized I shared the sentiment. If time passed, and people came and went, why expect anything? Why offer anything? The smart move was to take what was offered in the present and not expect much else. All of a sudden, I realized the difference between my old girl and Gypsy. My ex had been solid, predictable even. I had no idea what to think of Gypsy. I considered her as likely to be lying about the orphanage as not. That act in the restaurant proved she had her own agenda for the night. Still, I didn't care enough to dig into it. With the concrete calling, I didn't have a whole lot to lose. I just needed to keep my head out of the mix. It rarely proved more capable of handling a situation than my lower half. Fleetingly, I pictured her writhing on the floor, squealing under the weight of me. It took seconds for the image to take effect down low. I loosened my belt and readjusted. I hoped not noticeably. She sucked on the air. I could tell she was on a smoking binge, ready to pull out another as soon as she finished the one in her mouth. I decided it best to lift the mood and offered to smoke her up. Her eyes twinkled as she accepted.

I reached for a small pocket on the inside of my coat. I'd been thrilled to discover it. Perfect location, down around my hip, barely noticeable. I made frequent use. I asked for one of Gypsy's papers. I'd exhausted my supply earlier when I thought I was enjoying the last joint I'd ever have. As I rolled a new one, I briefly panicked thinking I might have botched my only chance to end things. I calmed down however, realizing a somewhat obvious truth. Anytime I decided to kill myself, chances were I could find some way of doing it. Comforted that death was at my beck and call, I licked the joint shut and told Gypsy to start us off.

It's always a sensual experience, that first toke, especially in mixed company. People's facades break down, a sense of camaraderie filters in. If only for those brief moments of anticipation, everyone's on the same page. Brains about to get lifted. Life about to get bearable. I watched Gypsy wrap her lips around the tip and gently breathe in. She held onto the smoke so it crawled down her throat and into her lungs. Then she softly let the smoke escape out into the night. She handed me the joint and our fingers touched. I lingered. A smile shone in her eyes, though her lips hardly moved. My chest constricted. I withdrew and focused instead on the pot. Took my time with it. I wasn't ready for an honest exchange yet. That look of hers recognized the challenge between us and called for us to keep moving. Keep pushing. Play out the fantasy for every last cent's worth. I took a deep drag and noticed the river had emptied. The boat had disappeared. Nothing new on the horizon. The city felt deserted, save the two of us. I sighed the smoke out. No safe word and no direction in sight, I thought. And the stakes were about to change.

Conversation grew out of the silence and eased along comfortably. Nothing of note, just vague observations that sounded increasingly insightful as the minutes ticked by. Somehow we got on the topic of how every few blocks constituted a different neighborhood in the city. Totally divergent populations laying claim, four blocks at a time.

The granny bakeries of Yorktown. The bodegas of Spanish Harlem. The crap retail on some avenues, the high-end designers on others. The money pits of Soho. The tourist traps of Little Italy. The theme park of Times Square, and the wretched streets around it. We split opinions on the Village. She preferred the West for its music, its food, its history. I argued that the area was just a bunch of ex-hippies turned capitalists eating overpriced brunch on Sundays. All the worthwhile culture had relocated to the East. Gypsy disagreed. She contended the West had plenty to offer, not the least of which was a sizable population of transvestites. Throw a rock and you'd hit four sex shops. You could buy a bong on any given street corner. Tattoo parlors were a dime a dozen. I stopped her there and challenged her to find a transvestite. Go ahead and try, I said. All we're going to find is wealth. She accepted, we said our goodbyes to the river, and walked to find a cab.

Didn't take long. Soon enough we were coasting through greenlight after greenlight, timed to perfection. Around Hell's Kitchen we started getting the munchies and decided on a mainstay of West Village culture, one even I couldn't discount. I leaned forward and gave the driver the slight adjustment to our destination. For some reason he started yelling, I couldn't identify the language. After a moment I noticed he was wearing an earpiece to a hands-free cell phone, but there was no guarantee it was on. I heard him use a spray bottle out of sight. Figured it was air freshener. Then a rank smell wafted into the back seat. Like rotten fruit and soiled sheets. I asked Gypsy in a low voice if she could tell what it was. She said she didn't smell anything. Then I watched as her face puckered up and her eyes lit with horror. In mere seconds we were both in hysterics. We rolled down the windows and a freezing wind whipped through the cab. That sparked a whole new fit of screaming from our driver but we pretended not to notice. Gypsy clutched her ribs, aching from laughter. I couldn't break from watching her skinny frame buck and collapse against the torn cushions. The storefronts blurred in the background, streaking yellow and red lights together like an underexposed photograph.

Do I have something on my face? she asked, catching my eye.

You're fine, I said, turning to look out my window.

The cabbie barked at us to pay the fare before he'd even reached a full stop. I gave him a twenty and asked for three back. He took it and continued ranting, English this time but in an indecipherable accent. After a minute I gave up and left without my change.

Our destination was a falafel joint on MacDougal, as legendary as anything left from the neighborhood's glory days. Tiny as a closet, no rhyme or reason to serving customers. We slid against the wall with the rest of the line, dodging arms as they shot through us to grab a handful of napkins. There was room to fit six people sitting inside. Outside the entrance, a few were crowded around standalone tables. We got our food and went to join them. Somehow managed to down a falafel each, plus an order of grape leaves and baklava to split. All the while my knuckles stiffened and my jaw clenched tighter from the cold.

Gypsy ran through most of the napkins, near-obsessively wiping the chalk white hummus from around her mouth. I grabbed some more, ducking through a couple body builder types wearing leather and eyeliner. Gypsy raised her eyebrows when I returned. I told her they didn't count.

You know how most girls would be saying how they never eat this much? she asked, downing the last of the baklava.

I grunted a response, busy thinking how good the honey would taste off her lips.

Well I say to hell with that, she continued. That was one good meal.

Full now, or you want dinner number three? I asked.

Right now I need some booze.

I'm sure we can find someplace, I said. Nearly every building around there had a bar on the ground floor.

We headed down MacDougal, poking our heads into the fuller places for signs of a good scene, ignoring the emptier joints altogether. We came across a bar aptly called Off The Wagon that sported a wall full of AA chips. She asked the bouncer about it, who said recovering alcoholics got drinks free for turning in their medallions. She glanced back at me and said it had potential. I told her to keep moving.

Half a block down we heard the thump of drums and bass. We tracked it to a grimy basement club and decided to give it a shot. I paid our cover. Our hands touched as we walked in. Her fingers were pale and soft. I wanted desperately to run my tongue between them.

There were a guitarist and drummer playing on a make-shift stage, no more than ten feet deep and six across. Their music was so intricate, so thick, it sounded like five members playing. They threatened to lift the roof off the place. It was dirty growling rock and everyone there was dancing. The place was packed and we were pushed together. She twisted her hair up around a pen. Her long neck caught the colored lights. She looked at me with eyes at once hungry and broken. My hands found her waist and she didn't resist. My body swayed in rhythm with hers. I pictured kissing her. More than once I licked my lips to make a move but something would stop me. Someone bumped into us. A song ended. My cowardice got the better of me.

Between sets we stepped outside for a cigarette. The chilled night air found the sweat on the back of my shirt and I shivered. She rubbed her hand over it, a smile on her lips. Tenderness. We smoked quickly and raved about the band. My throat burned but in a good way. My skin prickled and my head felt like cotton.

We stayed until the end of the band's second set. It had been one of those sudden discoveries that I heard happened in smaller cities like Santa Fe but never in a place as busy as New York. The band filled the club bit by bit until we were pressed against the walls, a mob of people continuing to arrive. I had the impression most of them were like us. We didn't know the band's name. It wasn't an ad campaign that made us come. We were just passing by when their sound filtered out onto the sidewalk and hit us like a drug. The music itself reeled us in. Gypsy called me out on it. Called the whole thing magic. I reminded her we still hadn't found a transvestite.

Gypsy led us down streets that curved and split so often I swore we were circling ourselves. We crashed in laughter on the steps of some brownstone. Looking up, I noticed that both street signs at our intersection said Waverly Place. How can a street intersect itself? I asked.

It's the nexus of the universe, she replied.

It's the West Village, I countered.

We developed a theory that the streets were continually shifting, like the stairways at Hogwarts. The evidence was compelling. Bleecker went vertical. Seventh Avenue went horizontal. When you came to West 11th and tried to head west you hit West 4th Street. If you headed the opposite direction you still hit West 4th Street. If you kept heading one direction long enough you ended up in Ghana. Conclusion? The West Village had charm. You had to have charm to have a Gay Street.

I paid for quality stuff and it was truly worth it. Hours after smoking and there were still cracked fireworks in her eyes. I mentioned them and she pulled eye drops out of her bag. They did nothing to hide the evidence.

You think there's anyone awake in these buildings? I asked.

It's not that late, she said.

What time is it?

High-o-clock.

She lost her breath giggling and her face settled into an exhausted smile. You don't know any good dead baby jokes, do you?

Of course not, those are sick.

Good, that was a test. I was testing you, Jumper. And you passed with flying colors. It's horrible when people make jokes at dead babies' expense.

I completely agree. It takes a real sociopath, you know?

Poor dead babies, she said, shaking her head.

... Well, it's not like they actually can hear us, I ventured. They're dead.

And even if they weren't, they're babies. They wouldn't even understand.

Too young, I said.

Too stupid, she said, correcting me. I mean, come on, dead babies, it's English. The easiest language in the world. It's not, like, Mandarin.

I had to laugh. She was higher than anything and falling asleep where she sat. Eyes half-closed. Sitting at a tilt. I cleared my throat and asked, You know why test-tube babies are the most beautiful ones?

Her eyes shot open. Why?!

Because they're hand-made.

She grinned. What's worse than smoking pot with a baby?

What?

Making a bong out of it.

What do you call a dead baby with no arms and no legs hanging on your wall?

What? she asked.

Modern art.

What's the difference between a dead baby and an onion?

What?

You don't cry when you chop up a dead baby, she said, grinning.

Why do you need to use a pitchfork unloading a truckload of dead babies?

Why?

So you can find the live ones on the bottom.

She sat up and cracked her knuckles. How many babies does it take to paint your house?

I don't know, how many? I asked.

It depends on how hard you throw them!

Okay, okay, I started. What's more fun than strapping a dead baby to a clothesline and spinning it around at fifty miles an hour?

What?

Stopping it with a shovel.

When is the best time to bury that baby you killed?

When?

When it starts talking to you again, she said, creepily waving her fingers in my face.

What do you call a dead-baby hobbit?

What?

Precious, I hissed in the Gollum voice.

She laughed so hard she farted. Not loud or obnoxious but kind of cute. Just a little toot into the air. I made a point of consoling her but she blushed little spirals on her cheeks. She called the last joke a cheap shot, said she had a crush on Frodo. The exhaustion hit her again and she wilted in front of my eyes. Move your arm, she said.

Why?

So I can lay down.

Oh, I don't think I can do that.

Why not?

You called me a cheater.

You are.

No pillow for you then.

Pleeeeeze?

Sorry, closed for business.

You know you want my head in your lap anyway.

I moved my arm. She plunged her head down and proceeded to toss and turn. Comfortable? I asked.

Almost, she said. Rub my stomach.

Sigh. Like this?

Over here more.

I obliged and we fell into silence for the first time since the river. The streets felt strangely empty, although I was admittedly too far gone to tell people from lampposts. Before long I got bored. Gypsy?

Yeah?

You really going to sleep on me?

I'm just resting my eyes.

So am I just sitting here, or…?

It's quiet time, 'kay? she yawned. Quiet time for Jumper…

I watched two lampposts pass and disappear smoking along the avenue. I heard quick pops forming a rhythm and realized with a groan that I'd started beat-boxing. Soon I was free-styling as only a white-boy could. Late at night / Mist in the air / I go there / To the place / Without care / Or struggle / On the face / Of the human race / And I change my pace / From fast to quick / And I feels so slick / When I gets in the thick / Of Waverly Place.

Jumper?

Yes?

Shut up.

I thought you wanted to sleep?

Ugh, fine! she groaned, sitting back up.

You can still lie down. My lap still felt her warmth.

No, I lie down I'm going to sleep. Give me a topic and I'll speak.

Politics?

Bush sucks.

Pause. Was that all?

What's up with the horse?

I turned to where she was looking. A rocking horse sat in a tall pile of black trash bags, its face turned our direction like a parent supervising playtime. Gypsy leapt from the stoop, dragged it out. A couple bags crashed and split open but she'd already started rocking madly. Her tangles flew up in the back and forth. A brightness hit my chest and it wasn't the pot.

You should totally stick this in your place, she said excitedly.

I am not going to be one of those people that fills their apartment with stuff they found on the street.

It's so cool though, she said, squealing. You can so tell somebody loved this thing.

It's in the trash.

You're looking at it the wrong way. Someone loved it for a long time and it got worn out is all.

Then why did they throw it away?

I don't know. Maybe the kid who owned it grew up and didn't want it anymore.

I didn't answer. Why was there pleading in her eyes?

You should take it, it would bring a totally new feel to your apartment.

I wouldn't know where to put it.

So get it up there and figure it out.

She stood, crossed swiftly, and knelt before me. Before I knew it her warmth was flooding through me. Her lips tasted like peaches. Her tongue spiraled against mine and fractured whatever shred of reality I had left. I grabbed hold of her. Her fingers crept inside my jacket. The tension disappeared from my shoulders, the weight in my heart lifted. I was struck warm, deaf, and happy. In a whirlwind we parted, grabbed the horse, and headed to an uptown avenue. We wedged the horse into a cab's trunk and climbed into the blissfully heated back seat. I gave the driver my address and linked back up with Gypsy. He eyeballed us in the mirror but we kept right on going. What could have been seconds later we were back uptown and racing into my building. In the elevator she ran her nails over my back and kissed the small of my neck. If I hadn't been holding the horse I would have jumped her right there.

Imagine the stories behind this thing, she whispered, inches from my ear. Maybe it got passed around from family to family. Thousands of smiles, only to end up in the trash.

That's not true, I said. It ended up with us.

She laid her head on my shoulder, the elevator approaching my floor. If I have kids I'm going to spoil them rotten. Give them candy, toys, whatever they want. Kids need that.

The doors opened. She reached in my pocket for the keys, lingered a moment longer than necessary, then pulled them out. The lock clicked and we went inside.

Your mother phoned while you were out, Gypsy called, skipping over to the wine rack. She selected a bottle and went into the kitchen to open it. Over her shoulder she called, She was wondering if we're still meeting her on Sunday.

I set down the horse and let out a sigh. No matter what I'd been hoping, it seemed the game was destined to continue. I don't remember saying we'd meet her.

I left a note.

I didn't see it.

Maybe if I taped it to your forehead.

Maybe, I said, under my breath.

You're going to have to introduce me sometime, she said, pressing on.

I lit a cigarette and sat down on the horse. My ankle was pulsing again. I fingered it. Raging stiffness. Cracks and pops. Big as a grapefruit. Nothing the wine wouldn't fix.

You were just going to let me look in here, weren't you?

I saw her expression and realized the corkscrew was still in my pocket. I tossed it to her. It bounced off her hands and clunked to the floor.

She picked it up, knifed off the wrapping, and twisted the screw in. I told you the horse would grow on you.

Like a fungus. I glanced at it under me. It rocked slightly in one direction and I widened my feet to stop it.

You like it.

If you say so.

I do.

I dragged on my cigarette, appreciating how she talked in statements rather than questions. The wine popped open and she slid out of her coat, reducing her to a wife-beater and that long patched skirt. Her navel exposed. I pictured tossing her tiny frame on the mattress just through the door. She grabbed two tall drinking glasses and filled them to the brim.

She asked a question but my mind was elsewhere. She repeated, What should I tell your mom?

You two are talking now?

Sure, when she calls.

You're here too much.

Do you not want me talking to her?

Doesn't matter.

I was trying to be nice, be the good girlfriend. Is that not alright?

It's fine.

Where do you see this relationship heading? she asked abruptly.

Groan. Can you bring the wine over if we're going to have this conversation?

I want to talk about this.

I'm not saying we can't, I said desperately.

She held the wine back. So talk.

I considered begging but thought playing along might prove quicker. I like you a lot.

... Is that really your best shot?

I rose and hobbled over but she avoided me, wine in tow. I'm really happy with what we have.

Did you ever learn to blow smoke rings? She demonstrated curving her tongue like a whale and keeping her lips round. I am so awesome.

... Can we drink now?

She teased the glass in the air, just out of reach. I don't know, Jumper. A dozen top shelf bottles and only cup of noodles for food? I think you might have a drinking problem.

It's only a problem if I don't do it, I said. The flask was empty and the red in the glass was calling to me. The teasing had lost its appeal and our moment on the stoop was all but forgotten.

Don't say I didn't warn you. She finally handed me the full glass and its weight proved comforting. What should we drink to?

How about to unwavering pessimism, unrelenting sarcasm and never-ending despair? I clinked my glass without waiting for a reply and downed the pint of wine in one go. Its warmth spread and I sighed in relief. Then I set the empty glass down on the counter and went to refill the flask. I brushed my fingers over the bottles in the cabinet and settled on the scotch from earlier. At least then she won't enjoy it, a voice told me. I had never been good at being teased and felt anger gripping my stomach. It tied back to St. Christopher's Elementary. The other kids never let me forget I had to commute more than hour each way, that I was a bastard because my father left. I held out as long as I could but eventually it came to blows. I chose the biggest of them, a good six inches taller than me, and started swinging. In sheer power it took five of my hits to match one of his but the advantage was all mine. I was the one with something to prove. Both our noses were busted, our eyes blackened. I ended up with a deep cut across my cheek that left a scar. But I was the one left standing.

The flask topped off with an ounce left in the bottle so I swallowed it down without a thought. Other than the heat in my throat the wine had yet to settle. In my frustration I'd drunk enough to take myself out of the game. In the moments before it hit I figured I better patch things up with Gypsy. She had gone to stand at the windows overlooking the green. I noticed her wine set down with plenty left but thought better of it. I came up from behind and slid my hands around her waist. She made no move to retreat so I kissed the back of her neck. I had a general idea of what I was going to say but the taste of her skin took control. I pulled the strap of her beater to the side and traced my lips along her shoulder. My other hand cut across her stomach and pulled her against me. When we did speak it was in monotone whispers, as if miles away.

It's a good thing you have an elevator, she said. Otherwise staying here would suck.

It's better than your place, with the mattress on the floor, I replied, kissing her back.

Quit bitching.

The day you get a box spring is the day I stop. My tongue reached the curve of her neck and she contracted. One of her hands found mine by her waist and gripped onto it. The other she lifted and ran through my hair. I began to lose track of my surroundings. I concentrated on her voice.

I want to open up my wings and fly all through this city, she said. Fly in between the buildings, over the streets. Fly straight into people's apartments, have conversations with them. I want to wear myself paper thin with all the love I bring to people.

You can do whatever you want, I answered. You're magic. Her hand tensed around mine and pulled it roughly into her stomach. Her breath wheezed out like a dying animal. I tried to pull away but she wouldn't let go.

I want you to hold me so hard I can't breathe. I want to disappear. I want something nobody has ever had. She spun, gripped the sides of my face and brought me into a harsh kiss. Suddenly I had trouble breathing. She wouldn't let go. Just kept hitting her tongue against mine. Finally I pushed her off. She hit the window with a thud and stared back at me.

I refused to think of the glass breaking. Of her body spiraling downward. Of the release I wanted for myself. I looked into her eyes, took comfort in her shortened breaths, then steadied myself and took her hand.

Her palm was cold to the touch. I laid it against the stubble on my cheek and brought my own hand to the nape of her neck. Our lips touched and spread. I flicked the tip of my tongue against hers. Then I entered her mouth full and swam there. Our mouths lost the connection for a moment and a strand of cold air got in. Then more of it. I couldn't tell if it was the wine messing with my radar or some secret agenda of hers but soon the kiss turned cold and wet. I backed away while she stared after me.

Is that what you want? she asked. All mechanics and no passion?

There was tons of it, I said, turning to my flask. A long sip, a lasting burn.

None to speak of.

If you didn't feel it that's your problem.

The new wave of drunk hit me and suddenly my voice was coming out different. I caught my reflection in the window and it surprised me. For some reason I'd been expecting to see my father. I heard nonsensical wailing and suspected it was me. I jerked my head around to see if she noticed but lost track of her. Must be in the bathroom, I consoled myself. Must be in the bathroom, I repeated in case I missed it. I found a vacant set of eyes staring back at me through the window and said the phrase a third time for good measure.

Do you see that homeless guy down there? a voice came through. I felt a dull friction and slowly understood I was lying sideways on the floor with my face pressed up against the glass. We should give him your rocking horse, Gypsy said.

I'd yet to locate her but hurried to prove that I was in no way drunk. I rehearsed my answer a few times in my head, making sure all the syllables were correct. Why should we do that?

It might make him happy.

Happiness. Is an illusion.

You're tough... Everyone deserves a present sometimes. Do you think he'd like the rocking horse?

I felt the darkness creeping up inside me the way it always did just before I passed out, growing out of my stomach with a warmth that was both poisonous and reassuring. An old friend that stole the best parts of me and left me ruined. A friend I couldn't live without. Except this time I was determined to stay with it. Stay with her. I paid my money and wanted my magic. Soon I was talking a blue streak.

What's he going to do with it? It serves no function. He doesn't have a roof. He doesn't have a shirt. And you want to give him a rocking horse to decorate whatever sidewalk he's laid out on.

You angry about something?

No, I shouted.

Yeah you are.

Look, I'm not even close to angry. If you ever saw me angry believe me it would scare the living shit out of you. Far off I fidgeted with pajama bottoms. I tip-toed frightened down a hallway. Gypsy taunted me. Someone else yelled. The hallway ended. I heard a crash. I was terrified of what was around that corner.

Keep me from flying. Keep me in a cage.

What? My voice was so sloppy.

That's what you want. She shoved me and I stumbled backward. I didn't remember rising to my feet.

What are you doing? I coughed.

Own up. Another push.

I'm sick, I told her.

She kept right after me. You don't want me to spread my love around cause if I did there'd be none left for you. Shove. Own up!

I don't –

Smack. My face stung hot where each of her fingers had connected. My mouth was running. Lord knows what I said to her. Own up, she repeated over and over. Nails dragged across my face. One pierced my eyelid. She ripped the hair from my skull. She grabbed me down there, tightened her fist and twisted. My adrenaline kicked in. I felt no pain.

In a flash the yelling in both worlds cut out, leaving only silence. My mother's legs stretched from behind our old couch. I knew she was awake by the way they shook. I stared at my blue pajamas with red airplanes on them. Set against the puke beige rug they looked like they were flying. My father's large shoes appeared and I followed them to pressed slacks, an untucked button-down shirt, a belt buckle peeking out, cuffs rolled, wrists exposed, fists clenched, forearms covered in curled black fur. That's as far as I dared go. The body was heaving. Then it brushed past me and disappeared.

My right hand hurt and I couldn't figure out why. With effort I uncurled its fingers to twist open the mouth of the flask. I forced the scotch down and followed its silent progression down my throat. I listened for a splash. I caught sight of my father in the window and smiled viciously. I mumbled curses at him. Vowels proved much easier to handle so at some point I started howling. Apartment windows glittered across the square and I desperately called to them. My throat wrenched open. It was a large wound and the louder I became the more it bled. I cried and laughed the next moment only to choke on my breath and cough up on my shirt. With a start I realized I was still wearing my father's dress clothes and tore at them like a murderous dog. The tie was first. I strung it up like a noose and pulled until it got difficult to breathe. I fingered the knot for a while and finally it loosened. I checked in with the vacant eyes and confirmed that our resemblance had diminished. I pawed at my hair and yanked off the jacket. I tore open the white shirt and left it hanging limp. I listened for buttons landing on the hardwood floor. Too much blood in my head. I blamed the wine. With relish I pictured planes crashing into the buildings outside the window and my father's shadow come flying out from the smoke. Landing on the pavement. Bones crunching, organs splattering apart, sidewalks swimming in his blood. All in slow-motion. My body was heaving like my memory of him and I tried to calm myself. Free me from his legacy. Craft my own destiny. Fuck up in my own way in my own time without throwback to the bastard that had flattened my mother in front of her own son and left them both the next day. Then I saw Gypsy's legs stretched out from behind my reflection and limped to survey the damage.

She had crumpled like a shot bird. With difficulty I resurrected the last few minutes. She'd been clawing at me and I grabbed her wrist. Then she bore her eyes into the part of me that wanted to squeeze so hard the bones snapped. I freaked out and let go. She slapped me again and I went for her throat. Her being so small my hand fit perfectly and her pulse throbbed against my palm. She sighed in short relieved breaths as if we were screwing instead of fighting. My mind went black but there must have been more. Around the apartment there were shards of broken glass. Overturned furniture. With a jolt I remembered her chucking objects across the room. The two of us yelling. That streak of violence I fought so hard to bury it killed me. I was so far gone I actually enjoyed the submission. She came at me and I flattened her full force. Closed fist. Square on her cheek.

Suddenly I heard knocking at the door. A voice. It took me time but finally I picked out words I knew. Mustering the best sober voice I could, I composed a response. In the end I had no idea what I said, what I thought. I sunk where I stood. I barely understood myself. Everything's okay, I slurred. Sorry for the noise. It's just the last of me dying. All that's left, is the body. Just the shell. Never a man. Worse than a kid. I'm dirty. I'm drunk. I'm heartless. Look at her. Her corpse on the floor. It's my fault. I'm the one. Too many corpses here. My father's. The Gypsy's. He's not in the pit. He's here. This apartment. Bomb it down. Bomb it down. I'll stay here right till the last. Father like son. You bomb it down. You bomb it down, got me?

I swung my head around to listen at the door but misjudged the distance and slammed right into it. Hurt like a mother. The room went white a second, then returned to the same old capsized vision of Hell. I prayed for god or the devil to give me a concussion. Whoever got to it first. I prayed to never wake up again.

I choked on a lump in my throat, hacked until the oxygen got in and straightened back up limp against the doorframe. Stared at the ceiling. Maybe there never was somebody knocking, I thought. Maybe there never was a voice. A terrorist attack. A Gypsy. Maybe I'd been tearing myself apart all along. That I could stand. That I could make sense of. With difficulty I rose to my feet and closed my eyes. Nearly lost my balance, teetering there. I counted three and opened my eyes, looking at the spot where I hoped there'd be nothing but hardwood.

I stumbled over and stood over her helpless. She'd gone limp as a rag doll, a red web forming where my fist had connected. Her patched skirt tossed inches over her knees. I saw the milk of her thigh and suddenly my head swam with visions. She would be my victim. I spent my whole life avoiding this but knew I could go that direction. Unless I could stop myself. I thought of the roses fallen across the steak knife. Of her rocking on the horse like a child. Of myself the way I'd always pictured but so far away now. I took a step back. Then another. And another. Soon my back hit the door. My hand found the handle and turned. With a final look at Gypsy busted on the floor I headed for the roof to end it once and for all.

Nathaniel Kressen

Nathaniel Kressen

CONCRETE FEVER

I lived alone with my mother for most of my life. When the uptown apartment opened up I jumped on it. No hesitation, no regret. No harsh feelings on either side. As long as I could remember she'd been a talker. Conversation perpetually one-sided, modesty dead, common sense nowhere to be found. I heard details no son should ever hear about his mother.

She went by the name Nix in art school. I subscribe to the Zen of Nix, she'd say, As in, nix that man we don't need it. She sat on the ground. Grabbed clothes off the floor. Slept at a girlfriend's place so she didn't have to buy a mattress. She hawked all of her family's furniture except an antique rosewood desk. She thought it was pretty. One afternoon a classmate called her on the double standard so she dragged a fork over it. Carved with the precision of a surgeon. Then paint, water, turpentine. It became driftwood. It looked ready to collapse. She treasured that thing for years.

For all the effort she spent trying to be a hippie she was really just a suburban girl desperate for an identity. That isn't to say she had nothing going. In studio she produced massive canvases filled to the borders with tiny ink sketchings, newspaper clippings, bodily fluids, bits of fabric, wood, metal, glass, you get the picture. No object was off limits and no detail was too small. She was That Girl At The Back Of The Class. It was inevitable someone took notice. An instructor, curator, buyer. Unfortunately it happened before they'd had an exhibition. The someone was my father.

What's the pus supposed to represent? he began.

Pus.

So it's a pus piece.

You should see my period piece.

I'm guessing we're not talking corsets.

We're not, she said.

What's your name? he asked.

Why, so you can scream it while you're inside me?

I only scream my own name during sex.

You must be really good.

When I try.

Sounds like your portfolio.

Sounds like you noticed, he smiled.

That you're either a jerk or a genius depending on your mood?

He showed no signs of reply, just kept on smiling.

It's stuffy in here with your ego.

Sure it's not your ten feet of pus?

Not unless I hung myself from the ceiling.

Kinky.

Go back to your hole.

My father kept after her. Visited the back of studio like clockwork. He neither applauded nor criticized her projects, simply made crude observations attempting to get under

CONCRETE FEVER

her skin. It worked. She began to look forward to their talks. She put on make-up. Laughed at his jokes. Laid in bed analyzing the day's conversation, waited in agony for the sun. Some classes he delayed so she came up with excuses to leave her corner. Wanted to try a new angle. There was a draft. I'm hopelessly in love with you. When they finally made plans she made a point of telling him she was asexual. Had no interest in penises. The best he could hope for was friendship. He weathered it patiently. Something else was building and they both knew it.

When my father came to pick her up she stopped dead. You steal a Mercedes? My father shined his condescending smile, she got in, and they sped for parts unknown. You got photo ID? She said she did, scratched her arm. He wasn't looking at her. They were leaving downtown. They were in line for the Holland.

I thought we were grabbing dinner? she asked.

I was thinking we'd grab Mexican.

My mother hugged her knees to her chest. They tore through the first cluster of buildings and out onto the connector. She whiffed the marshes and felt carsick. She told him. He kept driving. She fixed on anything that would distract from the nausea. Windshield polished to perfection. Dashboard reflective as a mirror. Ashtray, radio, impeccably clean. Engine at a hum. Stick shift gliding, his blushing knuckles on the shaft. His other hand draped lazy on the wheel. She thought a thief's fingers would be taut, white, gripped in a seizure of nerves. Instead she imagined a bubble bath and his growl calling to her. His hands slipping off her socks.

You stole yourself a nice one, she said to interrupt her thoughts.

I didn't steal it.

Then whose is it?

Mine.

Bull.

My family's loaded.

Lucky you. She wasn't sure she liked their game anymore. There were too many unknowns. Where are you taking me?

Told you already.

Tell me again.

You shouldn't worry so much.

Give me a reason not to.

You get a crease between your eyes.

She reached up to check and found it gaping like a canyon. Had he been staring? She eyed him but he was smiling straight ahead. Goddamn him, she thought. If he rapes me I'm going to bite the thing off. The nausea rose up again. She rested her forehead on the window and stared out at the oil fields. Miles of them. She cursed anyone with a hand in it. She thought of the drive from the airport. Her parents and their premonitions. We warned you about New England. All you know is beaches and sunshine. Now look at you. Nothing but cold winters and tar ahead. Artistic spirit, my foot. Stupidity, more like it. You won't last till Christmas. She remembered her mother's cracked face and shuddered. That drive from the airport. Tried to think of something else but it kept coming back. The airport. What did that last sign say? Lightbulb. Her head whipped, his smile grew, she dry mouth swallowed.

Are you taking me to the airport?

Finally he turned to her. You said you didn't have class till Tuesday, right?

CONCRETE FEVER

***

My mother was raised in a north Florida town without so much as a stop sign. When her parents said beaches what they really meant were swamps. Sunshine meant the gray humidity that descended ninety percent of the year. Fog infected your shirt sleeves and her first paintings were speckled with sweat. After school she worked a bait shop counter and bought herself a rotating electric fan. She produced two paintings a night and hung all of them together on her walls. Soon there wasn't a square inch left. Her family teased the circus must have come to town. It did nothing to stop her. She woke in their modular home with only one thought in her head. Her experiments grew in scope. She stole pamphlets from the guidance counselor's office showing cool slate sidewalks and yankee architecture, high rise neighborhoods with galleries at the corners.

Originally she chose home ec over art class. Those were two of three electives offered. The other was woodshop. Barf. Not so deep down she blamed her mother's ineptitude for everything wrong in her life. The cramped overheated trailer. The dead-end town. The dead-beat stepfather. She set out to make herself a better woman. It was only after a pastry exploded that she gave painting a second thought.

When she entered her first class she caught the boys clumsily drawing penises and the girls snorting acrylics from the tube. She wanted to leave but retreated to the back corner. It was this or building birdhouses, she reminded herself. She set down her bag. Grabbed brushes, paint and canvas. Took the stool and stared blank a while. The canvas was so goddamn white. It dared her to do something worthy. Her hands shook so bad she accidentally squeezed a full tube of burnt sienna on the table. She pushed as much as she could onto a palette but there remained a brown streak that looked like a botched dump in the center of the table. Her fingers were covered in it. The canvas laughed at her. She heard her classmates, her mother, stepfather, everyone laughing their stupid heads off. She couldn't take it. She swung forward and knocked her canvas over. She didn't anticipate the sound. The floor was slick masonite and the wood frame hit like a rock. The class lazily turned around. She couldn't meet their eyes. She still hadn't seen a teacher anywhere. She crouched behind her station to pick up the canvas. The glaring white was murdered. In its place were jagged streaks where her fingers hit. She saw her hand was still coated and pushed her full palm into it. Retracted and a story blossomed. She swiftly returned to her stool. Set it on an easel and grabbed for more colors. Someone chided but they were dead now. There was a buzz in her ears. Everything dead but this. Some colors she smudged with her fingertips, some she flicked with the end of a brush, others she swept over the thing with a chisel. It was desolation. It was the end of the world. It looked like nothing, a hideous mess, she overworked it so much the colors blurred into a dull purple brown and her forty-five minutes of concentration were lost. She swore the next one would be better.

One day a voice broke her concentration. You're pretty messed up, huh?

Classmates had pulled this before. They left sooner if she didn't turn around.

You continue these at home?

You know I don't. Even among this set her family's poverty was a joke.

How would I know that?

What do you care?

Come on.

She was pissed. She started with a symphony. Now there were only blotches and stripes. She spun around saying, What do you want, asshole? then stopped dead. The guy was thirty-five and tattooed.

To teach you, if you'll let me.

I'm sorry, I didn't –

Save it. No apologies here.

No problem. Sorry.

He smiled, a dimple in his left cheek. When you see a canvas, what goes through your head?

She hesitated.

It's alright, you can tell me.

I get pissed.

Why?

Because it's like – never mind.

What?

No, it's stupid.

Tell me.

It seems superior. Or, untouchable. I want to destroy it. Rip it apart or something.

So why don't you?

What, like, for real?

Why not? he asked.

Cause it's an art class, she replied.

Let me get you a blade. He took a few minutes. By the time he got back she had fixed her hair. Here you go.

Thanks.

Can I ask you a favor?

Sure.

Don't tell your classmates. I have enough trouble with them eating the art supplies. She laughed. I'm Mitch by the way. She started to introduce herself but forgot her name. After a moment he smiled gently, turned, and left her to it. She turned to the canvas and immediately began carving the hell out of it.

Gradually she learned to paint a picture rather than destroy a canvas. Some days the colors united in a delicate alliance, other times they fought full force. Mitch snuck her supplies to bring home. Canvases, sketch pads, brushes, and most importantly tubes of paint in more colors than she could fathom. Eventually she learned many items were from his own stash. She tried to return them but he insisted. Didn't need them. Hadn't painted a stroke in months. He left Austin when his mother got sick and returned to the swamps to care for her. In truth it was only a matter of time. Horrible as it sounded, he was just waiting until she kicked it so he could return to his own life.

The time came to submit her portfolio to colleges. Mitch owned a high-end Pentax. They developed shots themselves and burned proofs in his bathtub turned dark room. They spent hours together. All in service of her work. Of the future she could so clearly picture for herself. They talked. She had never had anyone she could talk to. Then suddenly there was a successful artist interested in her thoughts, from the letdown of Presence after Houses of the Holy to the hype surrounding Star Wars. With him she felt cultured. She dressed and talked how she imagined his girlfriends might have done. He drove her home nights and didn't crack on her family's trailer. She had always been

CONCRETE FEVER

petrified what people might say. She avoided the situation like the plague. But with him she felt at ease. She waved when he drove off. Thirty-five isn't that much older, she reminded herself.

The envelope sat fat in her mother's sweaty hand. Ripped open. A pinched scowl on her face. You know what this says?

I don't know, that Ray didn't pay the gas bill? The envelope landed heavy at her feet. She picked it up, slid out the acceptance letter, looked up with joy and got smacked. Pleas, threats, accusations of betrayal. Tried to reason with her mother but no use. Finally she couldn't take anymore, burst through the door and ran out into the night. Only one direction.

Summer hit early. The air split open and a storm whipped at her sideways. Drops bruised like bullets. Debris like blunt knives. She was winded within a half-mile. Slowed to a walk. Swallowed deep breaths. Caught headlights. Got off the road and hid in sopping grass three feet high. She recognized the pickup when it passed. Waited a few minutes then sprinted up the road to the trailhead. The path cut through the swamp for a couple miles toward a service road by the interstate. She took it slow. Thought things through. She was heading to New York. Didn't care how. Her first choice school wanted her and she'd make it happen.

Cheeks scratched, hair limp, clothes soaking and suddenly transparent, she climbed the four steps and knocked on Mitch's door. Spill of light. Whiff of green smoke. A hand led inside. Long hot shower and a fresh bathrobe. She looked in the mirror for a long while and finally told herself not to chicken out.

He was sprawled on the couch smoking a J. She joined and shortly felt high. It was her first. There was Zeppelin on the turntable. Immigrant Song. She stomached her nerves and leaned in. A few mutters of how they shouldn't, couldn't, but soon enough they were. Robert Plant was wailing. Mitch was guiding her head downward. His fingers in her black curls. The drums were bursting her ears. He exhaled and his fingers tightened on her hair. Sharp pain pierced the back of her neck. She rose to steal a breath but he pushed her back down. The record was skipping. The bass was all wrong. The air was smoked and stuffy. Her chest contracted. She needed to breathe. She tried telling him but couldn't manage words. Vowels only. He was shushing her. Her lungs went empty and the room caved in. Black air, green smoke, white flesh. She coughed and sputtered when he finished. The smell was overpowering. He tried holding her down there throughout but she pushed off him and hurried to the bathroom. He called after her that it wasn't polite.

Mitch said there were sienna and umber freckles in her eyes. Looking in the mirror she thought they looked colorless. Flat and dead. She scrubbed until her flesh wore thin but no matter what she did she could still smell it on her. She remembered the safety of her bedroom. Her thick covers and her dozens of paintings on the walls. Then her stomach sank. She'd run away. She'd never see them again. Her family was livid, probably trashed them by now. There was no going back and nowhere left to run.

Since I've Been Loving You was playing. She emerged from the bathroom. Mitch was banging around the kitchen out of sight and asked if she wanted a grilled cheese. Her stomach turned over and she headed the opposite direction. She was suddenly filled with the urge to meet his mother.

CONCRETE FEVER

Perpetually asleep. A closed door. Off-limits. She turned the knob and the door creaked. She checked behind her, no sight of him. She pushed it open and slid inside. Now familiar black air. A faint smell of central air gone stale. And an vacant mattress stripped of its covers.

I got Gruyere and chili oil, he announced. It's good, you should have one.

What. The fuck?

Huh?

You said you were taking care of your mother.

Swallow. You went in there, huh?

What's going on?

She, um, kind of died already. About a year ago.

Why are you living here then?

She left it to me.

What about your career in Austin?

My career, that's funny.

You said you were –

I wanted you to think high of me, okay? That's not a crime.

Blank stare.

Look, you're a sweet kid…

A sweet kid? I just blew you, for Chrissake!

You're the one that wanted to, I told you we shouldn't.

Right, you were really pushing me off… She choked back a sob. Silence.

Look. I'm sorry, alright? he said, not sounding sorry at all. Maybe you'd better just go.

It's a hurricane out there.

Well I can't drive you, I'm stoned.

She grabbed her clothes still wet on the top of the washer and rushed out the door. He called she was still wearing his robe. She tore it off and chucked it in the mud out front. It sank there defiled. She walked naked to the edge of the lawn. Sobbing but the tears got lost in the rain. The storm picked up and her bare skin got the brunt of it. She walked like that for a quarter mile before the shock wore off and it made sense to slip into her soaked clothing.

She started tripping harder. Mitch said it was only pot. It could have been a weird reaction. Still, there was little reason to trust him. Trees rose up like soldiers. The air pushed her down to her knees. More than once she cried out a prayer. She hadn't been to church since grade school. She barely knew who she was praying to but she did it all the same. Colors sprung from the dark and begged her to stop and admire them. Another voice told her to keep moving. Music was in her head. She matched her steps to the beat. Her stomach convulsed. She fought to control it. Her body was lost. Her mind severed. One thing revived her. She pictured herself in New York. The apartment. The friends. The lofted studios and spankin' new art supplies. A new life waited. She only had to survive the storm.

The service road turned into a treadmill. Her feet kept going but every step drew her backward. She got dizzy. Sat down and stared at the splashing on the pavement. It would be a good life. Die like this. She thought someone called her name. Her neck was so stiff. It took forever to turn and look. By then they were gone. Empty woods. Sweet air. She heard a string of pearls break and scatter. She looked around and realized it was the rain. She'd never been here before. She never would again. Her thoughts crystallized. Everything made sense. Briefly. Then the wind picked back up and forced her flat on the ground. Face in the gravel. Something was stalking her. She could feel its heartbeat. She hoped, when it killed her, that it buried her in the mud. She wanted to feel its thickness grip her. She wanted to sink. She remembered the robe and laughed. His voice cracked when she destroyed it. She laid on her back and laughed until her voice got hoarse. She sipped from the storm. Wished it was honey. That would be something.

The hours passed like weeks. The rest of the world skipped over them like a broken record. Immigrant Song. Now she was the one wailing. Cold, wet, alone. She questioned all her truths. Her heart swelled with epiphanies. Her head shattered in paranoia. When she emerged she was only sure of one thing. She'd been invisible her entire life.

At last the rhythm slowed. The howling died out. She squinted at the sky. Daybreak.

She staggered along the service road. Realized in a few minutes that she overshot and had to double back. A pickup appeared and slowed at the sight of her. She was still forty yards shy of the trailhead. Tried to run but her legs gave out. Loose gravel lodged in her kneecap. The scrape stretched a few inches. She ran her finger along it, only a flesh wound. Brakes screeched. The truck towered over her. Felt like an apparition. Seemed impossible that anything so ugly existed.

She sat at the passenger window and took inventory. Two men. Fifties or sixties. Couldn't tell whose belly was fatter. Whose twang was harsher. Whose head had less hair. Capsized rowboat and fishing equipment in the flatbed. A cooler sure to be filled with beer. At first they tried getting information out of her. Then she drew the switchblade from art class. After that they drove in silence.

She waited forty minutes in front of the school before the janitor arrived. Somehow she was surprised he didn't live there. He looked identical to the building. His jowls had

Nathaniel Kressen

the same yellowed rust. His clothes had the same mildewed smell. Their bodies sank in all the same places. He didn't ask questions, simply unlocked and held the door for her. They walked side by side a few strides, then he turned down another corridor. She paused and looked around. She'd been there since seventh grade but that morning it felt foreign. She eyed the trophies and awards, the pictures posted up. She wasn't in any of them. She was always an outsider but nonetheless considered the school hers. Only now did she realize she made no impression on it at all. The nurse's office was open and she bandaged her knee. She pulled dry clothes from the lost and found. In the girls room she got at look on her face. Half wet dog, half phantom. She picked it apart. Weighed her features. Then she remembered doing the same in Mitch's mirror and the whole night flooded back. By then her tears were dust. The storm swept away the girlhood heartache. The emptiness gave her strength. She chucked her clothes from the night before. Stood tall. Then she patted the knife in her pocket.

Corpses cried out from the lockers. Blood shone in the fluorescents. She reached the art room and breathed in the fumes. Slid out the switchblade and cut arches in the air. Targeted his jugular. Stepped back as his body fell. Treasured his last rasping breaths. His apology moments too late. The clock ticked closer. She didn't have him till fifth period. He wouldn't have calculated an approach yet. She paced the room and wondered what kind of supplies they had in jail. She had no illusions. It was her word against a dead man's. She only hoped they'd let her carve up canvases the way he did. Ten minutes to go. She pulled out her self-portrait. She'd been pissed over it for weeks. No time like the present. She grabbed a palette, a handful of acrylics, her

68

own set of brushes. Before long she was stuck again. It looked like her, sure. Certainly more than anyone else's. But there was no soul. Just a flat collection of curves. Empty. I'm invisible, she remembered. Three minutes before first period. She set the tip of the blade on the canvas. Square in her left eye. Ready to pierce through and nix everything. Then she heard her mother screaming. Saw her stepfather checking her out. Smelled the stench of Mitch. Felt her heart sink. Her first hardcore crush. Busted. He couldn't have cared less about her.

Mitch was down the hallway when his students backed out of the classroom screaming. A crowd hovered at the door. He pushed through. The canvas blocked most of her. Closing in he saw a dark cloud growing on her chest. What are you doing? No reply. Her fingers reached inside her shirt, came out red and crafted blotted shapes across the canvas. He caught sight of the used blade next to her and swallowed. Is that blood?

She eyed him impatiently. Would you excuse me? I'm working.

Back at the nurse's office they dressed her knee proper. Earlier she'd just stuck a band aid on without disinfecting first. Now the pebbles were lodged deep and hurt like a mother on the way out. She toyed with the gauze on her chest, uncovered a glint of red and felt better. Still there. The nurse removed the sharp objects from the room and left her there alone. She watched drops trickle off the roof. The sun broke through the last of the clouds. Everything was in harmony. When the period bell rang the hallways filled up. The office door trembled from the footsteps and conversations outside. Nonetheless she felt a deep quiet.

Nathaniel Kressen

They disappeared like she knew they would and she went back to thinking about the big city.

She woke up. She didn't remember falling asleep. A woman from the principal's office stood over her. She'd never heard this woman talk despite seeing her around for years. She looked like a moth slowly getting its wings pinched off. Perpetual silent agony. Lofted feathered curls with a decade of dust. Heavy rimmed glasses, not a speck of make-up. Your mother is here to see you, she said. That is, the guidance coun – Mrs. Simpleton – would like to know if you're ready. To see her. Your mother. That is.

There was some measure of comfort knowing there would be witnesses. Her mother couldn't smack her. Couldn't heave too dramatically. She'd be forced to play the responsible parent. On the other hand the moment was fleeting. Once they left all bets were off. There was only one shot to make that meeting count.

I did it because I want to go to New York, she began abruptly. I got into art school yesterday and my mom and I had a fight about it.

Frantic looks all around. Her mother looked ready to combust. The guidance counselor recovered first. Is that why you tried to kill yourself?

I wasn't trying to kill myself. I wasn't thinking at all, really. But if I wasn't allowed to attend this Fall... I'm not sure what I'd do. Five minutes later her fate was sealed.

It broke the bank to head north. The college's aid did nothing to cover airfare. Apartment rental. The hippie girl who scorned possessions might have exaggerated her situation. It wasn't by choice she sat on the floor.

My father booked the trip on a whim for their first date. Not hard. His family had their own jet. Tequila in

70

CONCRETE FEVER

America is nothing compared to down there, he said as they walked across the tarmac. Here people drink the junk just to get trashed. Down there it's like a national anthem. On takeoff she dug her nails into the back of his hand. Only the second flight of her life. The paranoia didn't let up. Every tremor was an omen. Every announcement was a threat. She made her peace with god. Mourned her lost future. Nodded numbly when he consoled her. She swore a blue streak during the landing. She was convinced the pilot was drunk.

From there he navigated them away from the typical tourist spots to a hole-in-the-wall restaurant with life-changing cuisine. He ordered for them both in thick americanized Spanish. Her defenses wavered. She teased him, he took it in stride, they made small talk until the food came. Each course topped the last. They got tipsy off tequila and sangria. Before long the whole country was dancing. The hiss of maracas was everywhere. The taste of sugar and citrus lingered in her mouth. Her smile lit the road to an adobe home off the main drag.

No hotel? she asked weakly.

Told you, my family's loaded.

The electricity was out. They lit candles. A blessing in disguise, he called it. She said it was just smart planning. She tasted the sangria on his lips. Sweeter than before. They kissed against the wall for a while making no motion toward the bed. The pure happiness of it set her on edge. A discord of voices rose up. This is too good to be true. Something's wrong. You can't trust him. He doesn't want you. If he did he'd be pulling you to the bed. You're not good enough. He could have anyone he wanted. You're invisible. You're nothing. This is one cruel joke and you're the target. She broke away, sat on the mattress, and wept.

He knelt in front of her. We don't have to do anything if you don't want to.

I do.

Then what is it?

Do you even like me?

He put his hand on the side of her face. She leaned against it. He kissed her forehead. Nix?

Yeah?

You do realize I don't fly every first date to Mexico, right?

A gentle laugh. A tentative smile. She laid back on the bed and he followed. They stayed there side-by-side a while just looking at each another.

He referenced a scratch on her chest. She peeled back the neck of her dress and revealed a host of thin jagged scars. Together they shaped a heart over her breast. She told him about carving herself in the back of the classroom. Refusing to be invisible any longer. Tasting, if only briefly, the full rush of life being lived. She paused every so often and he would nod to reassure her. He wasn't just weathering her this time; he actually listened. He cradled her head and told her things he never confessed to anyone. The claustrophobia of wealth and the crippling fear it bred. He was empty inside. His life was all laid out. He was surprised as anyone at the quality of his sketches. Enlisting in art school was more rebellion than true interest. Even now he dismissed his instructors' approval. There was no way to avoid his fate. When they finally made love there were stars in their eyes. It went slowly and lasted a long time. He was the first man she had ever trusted.

The lack of birth control had swift consequences. In two months they were holed up in a doctor's office. The

same week a blizzard hit. The way my father told it, it was
that abortion that brought my parents together – and my
birth that split them apart. The former took place that
winter as the snow piled up outside. They stayed indoors
while she recovered and fed each other creature comforts.
Shaped the little inside jokes that would carry them for a
few years yet. By the dozenth cup of hot chocolate they
knew. He bent a paperclip and slid it on her finger. Too sore
for much else, they kissed tenderly until she fell asleep in his
arms.

Nathaniel Kressen

Nathaniel Kressen

I lost count of how long I punched the wall in the stairway. My focus was miles south soaked in tequila. I failed climbing to the roof. My ankle shattered on the first stair and I collapsed in a puddle. It took until almost breaking my fingers before I realized what I was doing. Punch. Burn. Punch. Burn. Punch. Burn. My nerves shivered up my forearm and into my skull. I could have stayed there for hours. Could have kept on swinging until I tore through the wall, crawled through the breach, and tumbled out into the cold black night.

Her tongue woke me. Felt like a slug in my ear. I swatted at it with my eyes closed and the back of my hand caught her square. She fell back against the stairs and out of focus. I didn't remember passing out. First thing to hit me waking up was a wrenching pain in my hand. I cradled it against my stomach. The fingers lit on fire and the knuckles went looser than jello. I prayed for the numb drunk to return. The only thing I had left was a case of the shakes and a sour taste in my mouth. She crawled toward me. Half her face was swollen. I groaned and tilted my head against the wall. I couldn't face what I'd done. There was moonlight spilling from a window near the exit to the roof. How close to oblivion I was. I'd have to drag myself up the last flight if I was going to see it through. My ankle was snapped to eternity. Hand blown to hell. All of a sudden she was on top of me. Pressed her lips to my fist. Started whispering to it. Hard to hear what. I was in dumb shock. Seemed to be a thing with her. The greater the damage, the gentler her touch. She locked eyes with me. The fury was gone.

She guided my hand to the bruises on her face. She winced but kept it there. It felt like ham steak. I wanted to knife it apart and fry it. Pepper it. Swallow down its juices with a side of eggs. Sunny side up. Yolks broken and swimming in the cooking oil. I smelled coffee. I heard an alarm sounding. It was like that with Gypsy. An ounce of reality led to a fantastical world taking shape.

My mind spun epic conclusions. I'd been sleeping. What if another attack had hit the city and we were the only two left? It'd mean a totally new life. A clean slate. I wouldn't have to hide anymore. I could live and be true to the darkness. Lie to the Nth degree and end up sharing more of myself than I ever could otherwise. Somehow, for the first time in years, I could achieve a delicate balance.

Everyone said it was going to rain tonight but there's not a cloud in the sky, she said softly. Just you and me and the moon watching down.

Give me a minute, I groaned. My voice was so harsh it scraped my throat. Sounded like gravel. I withdrew my hand from her lips. Realized I had spit on my chin. Reached for it but a split second too late. She wiped it for me herself and continued.

I missed you in there. Missed my drinking buddy. Want to come back, go shot for shot with me?

I stared at her, disbelieving. My head dropped to my chest and I forced it back up. I think I've had plenty, I said.

Come on. Whatever doesn't kill you, right? Her torn face was inches from mine. There was wet blood below her eye. For some reason I wanted to press my lips to it. She slid her legs along outside of my thighs and perched there straddling me. She ran her nails through my hair, harsh enough they bore into my skull. A sigh of pleasure escaped my lips before I could stop it. She ran them through another time. Her body had a cloud of heat around it. She weighed nothing. I imagined her floating up the stairwell and crooking a finger for me to follow. Instead she pulled out the flask and teased it against my lips. The night flooded back. I tried to escape but she pinned me there.

You were wrong about me. When you analyzed me way back. My family's not –

What's it matter? she interrupted. Have one shot.

Listen, I've had it with this thing. It's over.

Give me a reason.

You're kidding.

I deserve one.

You used me.

And you didn't?

I didn't want this.

I'm not responsible for your depression or whatever this is, so don't go trying to blame me for it. You want me to leave cause I touched something in you that nobody's touched before, and that got you scared. You think it's sick somehow.

It is sick. Look at your face.

It's the most honest part of you there is. Your hatred, your violence, your passion. Your love. All of it. That's what I want. Let all of it go, and I'll swallow every last bit of it .

She kissed me. Hard. I tried pushing off her but I was weaker than I could understand. Tried again, same result. The commands choked in my head. I couldn't control my body. She kept right on after me. Tongue running up and down my neck, over my shoulder and collarbone, the tickle got me shivering. She was light as air. I could toss her across a room. I had one good arm, that should have been enough. But it wasn't. It moved on auto pilot, finding every square inch of her. Her ass was tight as an apple. The knobs of her spine climbed on forever. The feel of her on my fingers was pure music. I wanted to swing my fists full out. Bite and tear at her with every ounce. Rip off her limbs and reassemble them all wrong. My chest felt like it was going to split apart. Shatter my heart beyond repair. My stomach flipped again and again. My throat welled up and it felt like I was going choke.

Finally she let me steal a breath. I need to know if this is real or not, I said.

She pulled off her shirt and thrust my face forward. The skin of her chest smelled like sugar something. Grapefruit. Vanilla maybe. Her fingers ran marathons over my skull. Does it feel real? I snuck my head sideways and answered Yes. She told me to trust it.

Soon she was on her back and I was lapping at her like a dog. Her bra slid up and hung limp around her neck. I ran my hands over her, then my tongue. Bit my gums around her nipples. Slid downward. Licked spirals over her bellybutton before getting shoved lower. I pushed up her skirt and found her wearing nothing. Briefly wondered how she hadn't frozen to death. Must have left her panties in the apartment, I reasoned. Came out here with a mission, I thought as I ate her up. The length of her gypsy skirt draped over my head. It was a tent. Miles into the forest. Not another life in sight. Wild dogs barked. Bats flew overhead. The silence of night stretched acres around. I was reborn. In a rush I felt her paws on me and the warmth of her came rushing back. I pulled the skirt up. Beads of sweat were dripping from my forehead. She wiped my mouth with the back of her hand and kissed me deeply. Then she undid my belt. I helped her through the buttons, climbed out of my suit bottoms, stumbled out of my drawers. She ran one hand along me and kneaded my chest with the other.

Do you want me? she asked.

Yes.

Do you really want me?

God yes, I panted. Are you sure?

Aren't you? She had full grip on me and I was about ready to pop. Some people said it was best to think of baseball at such moments. Those people were sad and pathetic. I found a healthy alternative. I thought of digging miles up inside her and feeling her cry out in blissful agony. The concept of power always helped slow the timeline to a halt. Competitive nature or what have you. I focused on her arching back. Her swift muffled breaths. I regained my composure. My shirt hung open from earlier and I tossed the tails aside. Then she laid back, pulled me forward, and led me inside.

The claustrophobia was what got me. It was like I'd been given some secret. I had no breath. The air was sucked from the stairwell. But I wasn't going to die. I had everything I needed. It could have lasted hours or minutes and it would

81

have been the same damn miracle. At one point she brought my injured hand to her chest. Softly eased the fingers open. Then slid them around her throat. The pulse felt too familiar and I started to pull away but she shushed me. Locked eyes and I saw a kitten. Could have purred for all I knew. Bottomline we had an understanding. Go blue and pull away. Until then anything's fair game. Meanwhile she tore chunks out of my skin. Bites up my neck. Deep infected scratches the length of my spine. All the while those same tender eyes. The rhythm kept us sane. The rocking back and forth. Kept it going even as we repositioned to avoid spilling down the stairs.

Her climax came with a shudder. She signaled me to release her neck. Softly laughed to herself. I joined in. She put two fingers to her lips, kissed, pressed them gently to my own. Spun us over so she was on top and rode me till I finished. Then I took two fingers, kissed them, and brought them to the bruises forming on her throat. She collapsed on top of me and only then did I realize I was still inside her. I started to apologize but she silenced me. Nodded to acknowledge it. Then fell limp in my arms once more. The light from above cast weird shadows across her back. Her hair was in knots. It smelled of pot and sweat. I rested there without one thought of dying. It had been months since I could say that.

Emotions, poetry, or whatever usually made no impression on me. I spent the better half of each day trying to get laid, but when it happened I couldn't forget soon enough. The tastes, smells, sounds, rhythms, all of it got washed away. Even the names. Wrecked an awful mess socially, but it wasn't like I had to answer for it. The impact of the attacks cast a long shadow. I might screw over one girl tonight, but tomorrow there'd be another willing to comfort me. There was always another conquest around the corner.

What did you do to your hand? she asked. Her head rested on my chest. Head to toe our skin was wet and clenched together.

Tried punching through the wall.

Smart.

Could have made it if you hadn't interrupted.

Was that what I did?

I didn't answer.

Let's get you fixed up.

Ankle's shot too.

I'm a walking pharmacy, let's get you inside.

Might want to get your shirt on.

No one's awake.

We separated and she helped me to my feet. Stumbled to collect the clothes scattered across two flights. If anyone came into the stairwell they'd catch us bare-assed to the wind. Kind of hoped someone would. Gypsy seemed to get hotter the longer I spent with her and I wanted to share the moment.

Sitting on the couch my mind was clear for once. I watched her skip about the apartment half-naked, a dumb smile plastered to my face. I protested when she tried to slip into her wife-beater. She smiled, threw it aside, gave me a swift kiss on the cheek and brought over her bag. She playfully shook it and I heard rattling inside. She set prescription bottles on the coffee table in no particular order, five of them all told. Each had a mixture of colors and shapes except for one on the end. She recommended three whites and a couple yellows for good measure. I'd never been one for pharmaceuticals but if the night taught me anything it was to follow wherever Gypsy led. For herself she shook out two pills from the vial on the end. Crushed them with the flank of a butter knife. Formed neat lines on the cover of an oversized picture book. Cuisine of the Caribbean. Mangos and papayas peeked out through the fine white powder. She rolled a ten dollar bill and snorted everything in quick succession.

Wouldn't want to cut the night short, she beamed. I reached for the vial myself but she shoved it back into her bag. Let's see how the others hit you first. She took a quick sip from the flask and jetted into the bedroom to search through the closet. It's Let's Meet Jumper time, she called.

I limped after her. This isn't my apartment.

Come on, haven't you ever had a girlfriend?

What do you think?

She kept searching.

I lowered myself onto the bed. Ran my good fingers over the ankle. How long until they kick in?

You'll feel them, don't worry, she said, pushing through the suit jackets. Next, she crouched to the floor and began chucking shoes out into the room. Anyway, this is what girlfriends do when they want to know who they're sleeping with. I'm doing you the courtesy of doing it in front of you.

I reached for a pack of cigarettes on the nightstand. So that's what a relationship is, I muttered while lighting up. Exhaled. Sweeter than honey. I'm usually more likely to kick a girl out of bed than let her do what you're doing.

Right, like you'd have the balls.

To share or not to share? I thought. The decision took two seconds.

There was this girl Kweighbaye, I began. Her family was from Nigeria I think. She was American, no accent. We spent most of the night smoking and talking out on the fire escape. Told me her name meant A Hard Year. Her parents actually named her after a year of famine, monsoons and political upheaval. She told me the name really defined her life. I nodded in all the right places, contributed a few one liners, because what else was I going to do? We smoked up and started kissing. Brought her to bed – less than five feet from the spot outside the window – and in that time she tensed up. Told me she was a virgin. An admitted coke enthusiast, mind you, and a bit more sources told me, but nonetheless a virgin with zero intention of losing it on a first date. I've never been one to push, so I turned over to get some sleep. She kept talking. Said she wanted to know me better. I told her I'd rather she slept on the floor than open up. She thought I was joking and climbed right down. Expected any second I would invite her back up. But I was wondering, what if I just don't? Two minutes passed in silence. She made some half-hearted joke and I shot it down. Tried again and I threw her a pillow. Told her the draft wasn't as bad in the kitchen and there was a spare blanket in the closet. I woke up early and found her curled up in the corner. I threw on a pair of shorts and jogged up Riverside. I waited there till the afternoon, just watching boats go by. Got a breakfast sandwich, went back to river. It was past one by the time I headed back. Found the blanket folded and a note saying I was a prick. You might of seen it, it's taped it to the refrigerator. Kind of like a report card.

You're not a prick, Gypsy said. No matter how hard you try.

I know girls who would disagree with you.

I'm not like most girls.

Nathaniel Kressen

I stubbed out my cigarette and reached for another. I realized I no longer felt my ankle throbbing. The pills must have kicked in. The room wasn't spinning exactly but things were definitely leaning to one side. You know what's weird? I asked. You're the first girl I haven't wanted to choke every five minutes, and you're the only one asking for it.

You have old man taste, you know that?

The clothes are my father's.

So what, you live with him?

Not since I was three. He's dead.

Bummer. Heart attack, stroke, murder...?

He worked in the twin towers.

Yeah, mine too. That's why I'm in the orphanage.

Shut the fuck up, I snapped. She paused. My words rang in the air, silence hanging heavy over us. I tried to soften my voice best I could. Look, just don't bring that into the game, alright?

What game? she asked.

I'm serious. Just... just don't, okay?

She studied me then said, You're a bad liar.

That's probably cause I'm not lying.

Why didn't you enlist?

Excuse me?

If my father got killed I'd have signed up for the Army. Fly over there and start scalping fuckers.

I remembered wanting another cigarette and searched the bed for the pack.

Didn't part of you want to? she asked.

Part of me? No. Part of me didn't. All of me is happy he's gone.

Wasn't exactly a model father, huh?

Suddenly I realized what was off. What did you give me?

What, you freaked out?

No, just... I've never talked about this to anyone. And people have tried.

It's the yellows. And don't worry, I don't think you're a pussy. Did you know there's a safe in here?

What? Oh yeah. I can't figure out the combination.

I got an idea. She skipped into the living room and was back with a handful of liquor bottles from the cabinet. If he's anything like you we've got our answer right here.

Can you hide those from me, actually?

Aw. Jumper has a hangover.

Jumper's in the middle of a bender, is what.

You seem pretty sober to me.

Fucking clarifies me.

Gypsy giggled. Complete, genuine laughter. Looked at me tenderly, then went back to lining up the bottles. I watched her a second, at a loss. Her tiny frame crouched over the bottles, arranging them with utmost attention. A little girl building sand castles on the beach. Somehow, until now, she'd been an idea. A reckless and dismissible ghost. But the hint of something underneath was enough to throw me. There was a teenage girl in there sure enough, with just as many ties to childhood as she had to being an adult. I let out a breath and felt the sickness fade. Then I followed her white hands to the bottles on the floor.

Their long necks flickered orange. I looked around and saw candles scattered throughout the room. I hadn't seen her light them. Now I couldn't stop staring. Just a couple weeks earlier a girl taught me how to control the energy in a room. Proved easy enough, just a matter of focus. I tried doing it, sprawled there on the mattress, numbly wishing at the flames licking upward. For a few seconds I got one. The rapid jerks ceased. The excessive movements quit. Just a slow methodical burn. A soft caress of the sky.

Alright, the first three letters, she announced.

I looked over. Gypsy was beaming. She'd even grabbed a paper towel from the kitchen and drawn a table with letters matched up to numbers. She reached for the first of the bunch.

Okay. Dewars. D-E-W. 4-5-23. Nope. Jameson. 10-1-13... Glenfiddich. 7-12-5...

Why don't you try A-S-S for Asshole?

Don't you want to know what's in here? Could be money.

I already have his money.

All of it?

Pretty sure.

And the will didn't say anything about what the code was?

I guess it wasn't important enough to mention.

Or too important.

Look, the soup's probably done. You ready? I got up. My ankle gave a little but the pain was gone. She didn't budge from the closet. You coming?

You're really not interested, are you?

I'm interested in a meal. I started for the kitchen.

... You tried your birthday, right?

I kept walking hoping she'd get the point. Instead she started shrieking.

You have tried it, haven't you?!

It would be a waste of time.

How do you know, though?

Because I knew my father. It's the last thing he would pick. I doubt he even knew it.

I leaned against the door frame, lifted the swollen ankle and tried drawing circles with my foot again. It looked like a fat capsized turtle trying to heave itself off its back. My stomach growled for something to absorb the liquor. I wondered if I had any bread to go with the soup. It'd be stale if I did. Hadn't bought groceries in weeks. Planning to off myself and stocking the cupboard didn't exactly go hand in hand. I looked back and saw Gypsy still buried in the closet. No sign of giving up. So I figured it'd be best to get it over with. The sooner it failed, the sooner we'd eat. I told her the date. She crouched. Dialed in the combination. And the door swung right open.

Told you I'm magic, she gloated. I went to look through the spoils. First thing to catch my eye was an aged bottle of Scotch. My stomach turned at the sight of it. Didn't stop my mouth from watering though. I picked it up and considered its label, its weight, maybe a moment longer than necessary. Gypsy lost her patience. You going to drink it or stick your dick in it? With a hard swallow I set it down unopened. Next was a collection of porn magazines. A whole host of genres. The first sported an absurd amount of production value. Airbrushing. Dramatic lighting. Tits no one could fathom as God's creation. You could hear the cheesy music. The magazine below was the polar opposite, amateur to a laughable degree. Underlit, underfed sex symbols bearing everything. The shots looked like they were taken in someone's living room. Gypsy and I flipped through the entire stack, occasionally cheering for a gang bang or turning a centerfold sideways to get a closer look.

Next was a watch. I'd always thought of a nice watch being those pieces of flash displayed in midtown storefronts and therefore had zero interest. But this had class. It had weight. Texture. Grease and soot between the links. It might have been a century old for all I knew. My eyes lit up like stars. Here was a connection I could appreciate with my father. A hint of something substantial. I was all set to put it on until I flipped it over and read the inscription. Turned out it had been passed down through the men in my family. Generation after generation. Father to son. My fist clenched around it, knuckles cracking. Gypsy tried to catch my eyes. Without a second thought I tossed the watch across the room. The silver spun end over end and landed with a dull thud on the hardwood. Rolled under a dresser. I made a mental note to forget all about it.

After a moment Gypsy took a stash of pictures from the safe. I pointed him out. She said I was the spitting image. I tried pocketing them but she insisted we look through. I agreed as long she made it quick. The first few were taken recently. I recognized his girlfriend from the funeral. She'd introduced herself. Tall. Unnaturally black closely cropped hair. Okay frame. Obvious inherited wealth. Slightest hint of crazy. Don't know what she'd been expecting from me. Polite smile, commiserating hug. I half-remembered staring at her blankly until she walked away. Wasn't out of spite. Not toward her at least. I was so hung over at the time that I'd put my boxers on backwards and spent most of the service readjusting myself. Would have thought it'd be obvious, but my extended family was too busy being angry at my mother for refusing to attend. When I'd left to catch a cab that morning, thirty minutes to show time, I'd found her incapacitated on the living room couch not breathing. Tried reviving her but no success. Took the phone and dialed an ambulance, get her stomach pumped from whatever damage she'd prescribed herself the night before. As if on cue she sputtered awake and gave a lengthy diatribe insulting the old man. Then she fell back asleep.

The memories from the funeral kept coming. Face after face. Some of his luckier friends from work. Relatives I half-recognized. Then came a set of older pictures turned yellow. Warped like they'd been handled too rough. A lot of them were of me as a kid. In those he had less wrinkles. Less heaviness in the eyes. The two of us were pictured at a playground. At a ball game. A circus. All the stereotypical places a divorced dad would take his kid on visitation weekends. In every one I was smiling. Ear to ear. Briefly my heart swelled, remembering what it was like to have a hero. To worship something. Anything. To believe that something good existed. My throat caught on the positivity and I buckled over. Room spinning, dry coughs wrecking my lungs, blood flooding my brain, I caved in on myself. I fought to breathe. To think of something suitably tragic to get things on an even keel.

Then I remembered waiting at the window for him to pick me up. I'd spend the day starving myself so I could eat as much of his cooking as I could. Standard comfort food but it meant the world to me. Spaghetti and meatballs. BLT's. Ice cream sundaes. More often than not, the rock in my stomach poisoned the air and emptied the streets. I'd sit there for hours, cramped up, crying. Sometimes he failed to show up at all. I looked past it a few years running, never held a grudge, but the dismissals never quit. Then, one day, after only the most mild provocation, I dismissed him once and for all. After that the most he got were brief face-to-face chats. Always a public venue. Never more than a half-hour. It was a chore, but he paid good money for my company. I stopped considering myself his son. I was his mercenary. His whore. His little wind-up monkey puppet. All he got was show. I never felt guilty about it, but I did wonder if he ever realized the extent of the farce I played.

When we were sure the dry heaving had passed Gypsy got me straightened up. Stroked her fingers through my hair. Rested her palm on my forehead. Finally the voices quit. She hid the rest of the pictures under some dirty clothes on the dresser. I stared at his shirts and suit jackets hanging in the closet. Besides what I'd chosen for the jump I hadn't touched anything since moving in. I wondered whether he did his own laundry or hired someone to take care of it. It was all was perfectly pressed. Not a wrinkle in sight. No stains or blemishes.

A chill ran over my back. Gypsy had cracked a window open and hung her head out to smoke a cigarette. I don't care if you smoke in here, I said.

I wanted some fresh air, she answered.

I put on one of his button-downs, then got one for her as well. Walked over and wrapped it around her naked frame. She curled in close. Breathed a deep sigh against me. We looked out. The sidewalks were bare. Not even our homeless friend from before. Hardly any cars. Just taxis and towncars coasting through.

It's so quiet, she whispered.

It's late.

You're not tired are you?

Nah. I'm up.

We in it for the long haul?

You mean till sunrise?

CONCRETE FEVER

Why not? We have plenty left of the game to play.

I kissed the back of her head. She shifted. Just an inch to the left, but it put her in the crook of my arm. We stood there not talking. The night opened up ahead. The rhythm of her breath told me everything. I felt her thoughts on the air. They floated there like dazzling lights.

***

The soup was standard fare. Two dollars bought six packets and even then it wasn't that great a deal. We wondered what random chemicals we were ingesting. In the end we decided our meal was one notch up from licking the pavement in Chinatown. Left wanting, we decided to go all out and order dinner for the third time that night. We looked up an all-night burger joint that also offered a selection of cigarettes. Gypsy got a turkey burger with jack cheese and a pack of Marlboro Reds. I got a pulled pork sandwich and an extra pack of Camels. We got tater tots to split.

Gypsy dolled up in anticipation of the delivery guy's arrival. Added a few grams of mascara. Lipstick so dark it looked purple. Unbuttoned the dress shirt to great effect. Loosened the top of her skirt so the crevices inside her hipbones were showing. Her hair was still a mess and her eye had blackened where I socked her. One of her cheeks had swollen. Still, as though nothing had happened, she bounced from the mirror to where I stood and gave me a deep kiss. She posed for one last check-over. Ravaged a la punk rock. A walking junked up corpse. Resurrected and back from hell for more. The door knocked and she motioned for me to hide. I circled a corner and watched the scene play out in silhouette on the wall opposite. When the door opened she draped herself on the doorjamb and spoke in her best raspy sexpot voice. The guy stammered a response. I heard a faint girlish giggle. Realized after a moment that it was coming from him and went into stitches. Had to cover my mouth to stifle it. In a stammering voice, he asked if all the food was for her. Some is for my boyfriend, Gypsy replied. He's handcuffed in the bedroom. With that she snatched the food out of his hand and slammed the door. We listened for a full minute before the elevator outside finally chimed. Its doors sadly closed and the car trudged the long trek downstairs.

Free food! she exclaimed. She dumped everything out on the table. The tots spilled onto the floor but we called five-second rule and ate them just the same. Mouthfuls of greasy, glorious meat later, we were blissfully satisfied for the second time that night.

You better get your strength up for round two, she reminded me.

Something down south did a jig. Ready when you are, I told her.

A broad smile spilled across her face. There was ketchup on her teeth. You interested in finishing off the safe first?

My stomach dropped. There was more in there?

Think so. Don't worry, I'm sure the worst is over.

We finished our feast and headed into the bedroom. I was going to let her take the lead but she flew into the air and bellyflopped onto the bed instead. She swiveled and sat there staring. Well? she urged. I hobbled over to the safe. The only things left were a couple bundles of letters. I took them out and saw they were all marked Return to Sender. Went to put them back but something stopped me. I looked closer. His handwriting spelled out the same destination over and over. I flipped through. There were dozens of them. Each and every one addressed to me.

What is it? Gypsy asked. For second I couldn't speak. She sat up. Jumper...?

Letters he wrote me, I said. But they never got delivered.

Wrong address?

No, that's my mom's apartment.

That's weird. Gypsy went for the cigarettes. Lit two and handed me one. I shook my head. She put her hand on my shoulder but I shrugged it off and took a step away. Something wasn't adding up and I needed to think it through. There's no reason to get worked up, she said. You're not a kid anymore. He's gone.

Yeah, I know that.

You don't have to snap at me, I'm only trying to help.

Okay, well how about letting me think?

Ease up, I didn't do anything.

I know that.

There's no reason to get pissed.

I'm not.

Well you obviously are because you're yelling at me right now.

Look... I was about to say something but thought better of it. I took a deep breath and started again. I'm going to take a second and figure this out, okay?

She looked unconvinced. Take all the time you want, nobody's stopping you.

I took the rest of the letters into the bathroom. For the first few minutes all I did was plan damage control for when I got out. When I finally looked at the top letter I got jolted. It was postmarked less than a month before the attacks. I tore it open.

August 14, 2001

Dear Son,

When Jill's on the rag it's like a freight train runs through this apartment. She's been after me about when we're moving in together and starting a family. I tell her what a lousy husband and father I made but she doesn't listen. She just says my mistakes are in the past, we need to give our life together a shot. I swear sometimes solitude might be the way to go. Maybe I should move somewhere and become a monk...

So it's still weird writing you when I'm sober. (90 days tomorrow.) All I can think about is how pointless it is. My sponsor says to write you anyway. He reconciled with his daughter a few weeks ago so now he's even more optimistic. Don't get me wrong, but I don't think you can rush something like that. It has to happen in its own time.

At the meeting tonight this guy with a bad toupee went on and on about the "skeletons in his closet." For fifteen minutes, everything he said was in metaphors. Got to the point no one knew what he was talking about. I had to bite my knuckles to keep from laughing. Made you want to wring his neck. Even so though, when he was wrapping up, he said something that actually got me thinking. And I know that everything's part of the process and it's supposed to be healthy to feel remorse but I don't feel like it's helping. It makes me want to buy up a whole liquor store and bomb the hell out of my brain for a few days. I know you won't understand. I hope to God you never do. But when you're my age and there are more

CONCRETE FEVER

opportunities behind you then second chances ahead... I don't know why I keep writing this garbage. It's not like you ever open them. I understand why, okay? And I don't blame you. But you have to give me a chance at some point. No offense, but every time we meet up I get the feeling you have one foot out the door. I can't figure out how to talk to you. Get a conversation started. It's been years at this point. I want to make an difference in your life.

If you feel like it call me. No pressure. I'd like to hear how your summer's going.

Dad

I reread the letter twice, then grabbed for the bundles at my feet. Flipped through and picked out the oldest postmark I could find. Did the math. It would have been the spring of second grade. When I slit the top open a baseball card fell out and landed face down on my lap. Turned it over and a rush of memories flooded back. With effort I turned to the letter. The handwriting was sloppier than the last and the paper had a hospital's letterhead.

April 21, 1993

Son,

I finally found you a Mike Piazza rookie card! Not many in stock yet, the printers don't seem to share your enthusiasm for the guy. I'm still laughing at the slice of pizza you drew onto your jersey. Just cause he has a cool name does NOT mean the Dodgers have a shot! Start rooting for the Mets already, they're your home team, bud!

Thanks for coming here to watch opening day. I know it couldn't have been fun with the volume turned down and the nurse checking in but it made me feel tons better.

I wrote you last week but the letter got returned for some reason (probably shouldn't have written down this room as the return address — hopefully the apartment works better). They're transferring me to physical therapy next week! It's great news. The leg's recovering sooner than expected and now they say I'm going to get the full range of motion back in my shoulder. So you better practice big man, otherwise next spring I'll be swatting down your jumpshot like always!

I'll give your mom the number for the new room when I move. Hope little league's going well!

Love, Dad

The bathroom stank of morphine. I fixated on the drawn shower curtain. Got convinced there was a body hidden behind there hooked up to all sorts of tubes and plugs. The leaking faucet rung out like the blip of a heart monitor. My eight year old self counted the rhythm with the obsession of addict. All of a sudden I couldn't handle it. I jumped to my feet but hesitated once my hand touched the door. I wasn't ready to face Gypsy yet. But the booze out there was calling my name. Too many memories were taking hold. I needed oblivion. I considered my options, then suddenly lost sense of where I was. I remembered long white hallways. Slick linoleum. The smell of sickness in the air. Fear tugged at my intestines. The place was so vivid I worried my bowels would burst open. I heard my mother break the news to me in that half-tragic half-oblivious way of hers. My father had had an accident. Hit another car and spun into oncoming traffic. He'd been driving high speed so the impact was rough and he flew through the windshield. She made it clear there was little reason to hope. Full recovery was impossible. He'd most likely be paralyzed. He might die on the operating table. I tried to drown her out but she kept listing the potential disabilities. I curled up to sleep but the waiting room chairs had narrow arms and my limbs cramped up. My mother paced and muttered to herself. A few hours in we got word he survived the operation. The medical jargon spilled from the doctor's mouth and it gave me a headache to keep up. The words vomited out like bile. I prayed he would exhaust himself and fall face down on the sanitized floor. All I wanted was to see my father. They advised against it. I protested. Didn't care what shape he was in. He was my hero and he was hurt and he needed me. It was as if I'd said nothing. My mother shot me down point blank and insisted we go home. I didn't speak to her for a full week. At last she took me to see him. When we got there I was sure we made a mistake. I paused to check the room number but my mother nudged me forward. I counted the floor tiles all the way to his bedside. Finally glanced up and found his brown eyes peering from underneath layers of white gauze. The operation left his head bandaged and the rest of him in a body brace. They wrapped one of his legs and suspended it in a sling. A cast stretched the length of his left arm and around his shoulder. His splintered bones would never fully recover. A pair of drill-holes would scar either side of his forehead where a metal plate had gone in.

When I managed to say hi, my voice shook. I stared out the window for most of the visit. I wet myself on the taxi ride home. Imagine the person you love most in the world had their skull cracked open and their face dyed yellow with iodine. Picture crumbles of caked blood falling from their hair onto the sheets next to your hand. Now give them a big hug and pretend it's all okay.

I jerked myself out of the nightmare. Chills ran through me. I took a towel off the hook and brought it around my shoulders. I buried the memory of seeing him for a reason but the rookie card brought it all back. I concentrated on catching my breath and getting my bearings. I had no idea how long I left Gypsy for. I figured she'd either stolen everything or been planning ways to torture me. I eyed the dozens of unopened envelopes. The first two had been enough to immobilize me. Part of me wanted to burn the rest. I'd decided to jump because I didn't have faith that anything worthwhile existed. But since then I'd been blindsided. These letters promised answers to questions I never knew existed. I couldn't open them yet. I understood that much. With a sinking stomach, I realized there was only one alternative.

While I was in the bathroom, Gypsy had been drawing in lipstick across the cupboards in the kitchen. Manic cartoons depicting the death and destruction of what looked like Smurfville. She'd drawn Smurfs getting lynched, impaled, electrocuted, crying for mercy. Gargamel cowered on all fours, bound and gagged, a dominatrix Smurfette cackling over him. When I came out of the bathroom she was finishing off a pair of muscular Smurfs sodomizing each other.

Howdy! she smiled. Hope you don't mind.

Not at all.

Hold on one second! She turned back to draw a cowboy hat on the giver of the two.

Place looks good.

Doesn't it? She capped her lipstick to give me her full attention. So?

So...?

You did a lot of soul searching, huh? Discovered profound new insights?

Well, I did come up with a next location. I waited for her to stop me but she just gave me a pure wide-eyed smile. I swallowed. You said you wanted to meet my mother, right?

Nathaniel Kressen

Nathaniel Kressen

Nix never regretted the procedure. She couldn't imagine cradling a child. She could barely comfort herself. Half the time she felt stretched too thin to exist. Still, the days stopped dragging. Her work in studio hit a new level. She made peace with the scar on her chest. Then, when she had finally let herself believe the happiness might last forever, her mother announced she was coming to visit.

She prepared for their dinner with a cocktail of red wine and Tylenol. In time she'd discover stronger combinations but at the time it did the job. Nix stared at herself in the mirror. Tried on each of her outfits, ran through them again. All the while trying to adjust the parts of herself that couldn't be adjusted. Her stomach sagged. Her tits were too small. Her eyes looked dead. Her arms withered at her sides. Knee deep in reject clothing, she finally settled on a long grey dress from the hamper and a pair of black leggings. Then she forced herself to use the red lipstick her mother had sent, and even added a touch of foundation. Absolutely not her style but she swallowed it.

Nathaniel Kressen

She wanted her mother happy and comfortable when it came time to tell her.

Nix met her mother near a subway stop in the Village. A homeless man with duct-taped hair was excitedly describing the glow of energy surrounding her. When they departed he followed. Nix finally got rid of him with a few choice words that mortified her mother, then led them both into the circular cobblestone streets.

Occasionally they stopped at a restaurant awning only to dismiss the menu as overpriced. They walked north, but remained unsatisfied. Their blood sugar dropped. They started snapping at each other. No outright insults, just the typical mother-daughter passive aggression. Soon they went silent altogether. In the end they settled on a chain restaurant recognizable from any suburb. When the onion rings came Nix stomached them like she did the make-up.

Her happiness means everything right now, she reminded herself. The woman who gave birth to me. Flew three hundred miles to see me. Who doesn't understand why I'm here. Who thinks eventually I'll come to my senses. Who refuses to recognize this is what I was born to do. Who cuts me down the second I try to better myself. Who thinks I'm worth nothing. Who thinks I could lose weight. Who wouldn't care if I ended up broken, alone, saddled with children. The woman who wants to see me fail so she can clean up the mess. That woman there with the spiced mayonnaise spilling out the corner of her mouth. That's the woman whose approval I desperately need... Hiding her disgust, she washed the salt and oil out her mouth with an orange cola.

Nix listened patiently as her mother spoke a full ten minutes on the virtues of moving home. Apparently the

106

neighbors had taken an interest. They were willing to pay for her to paint their mailbox. Full artistic license. Eventually they hoped to have a birdhouse as well. If the project went smoothly others might use her too. It could be a whole new life for her. Hometown artist makes good. And – here was the bombshell – her mother had been saving part of every paycheck to make the down payment on a house for her. Nix choked on her dinner roll. She remembered the claustrophobia of their trailer. The memory alone was enough to make her feel trapped. Yet here was her mother willing to put all of her savings toward a separate home for her. House, she cursed quietly. It would be a house, not a home. Her mother pressed on. She might have had trouble expressing it, but Nix meant everything to her. She'd never meant to drive her away. When the idea of New York came up she'd already been scouting houses. Move back home, her mother pleaded, and I'll help both of us get a better life.

I've met someone, Nix said.

You'll meet someone else.

Not like this.

What's so special about this boy that makes you want to give up a happy life?

There's no guarantee I'd be happy.

What are you talking about?! her mother cried. It's your home!

Nix glanced past her mother and saw half the restaurant staring back. She ducked her head, hoping her mother would take the hint.

Oblivious, she continued, You'd have your own place, everyone you know is down there...

I'm on a different path, she said under her breath.

You think you are.

No, mom. I'm sure of it.

You're young, you're not sure of anything.

Nix slumped in her chair and glared over the table edge at her mother. I still don't know how to talk to you.

Open your mouth, I'm right here.

You just –

Your problem is, you don't think about what you're going to say.

I do think. You just don't listen.

How could I not listen?

I got pregnant.

Dessert or coffee, anyone? The waiter stood over them awkwardly, his mouth forced into a toothy smile. Nobody answered. Eventually he slunk away. Nix watched in horror as the anger knotted in her mother's stomach, boiled up past her chest, turning her face and neck red. She waited for an eruption of some kind. The seconds dragged into minutes. The fury simmered there inside her, ready to explode. At last, in a voice much to quiet to be convincing, her mother said, It's alright sweetheart, we'll raise this child together.

Nix's eyes flickered. Her mother sat upright. She tried to recover. Maybe we should get the check.

Sweetheart –

Where's the damn waiter?

We should plan your coming home.

You should get back to the hotel.

I'm not tired.

Of course you are, you just flew in.

How far along are you?

I don't want to talk about it.

It's a blessing.

I really don't want to talk about it.

CONCRETE FEVER

I'm your mother.
I really don't –
We have to plan you coming home.
There isn't going to be any kid, alright?!
... What are you talking about?
I, I had a miscarriage.
Oh. Oh god, sweetheart. I'm so sorry. Of course it's not
the end of the world. Your aunt miscarried before your
cousins were born...

Nix spent the rest of meal listening in silence. On the
walk to the hotel her mother insisted she bring her
boyfriend to dinner the next night. In the lobby they shared
the obligatory hug, each willing it to mean more than it did.
Her mother paused afterwards with her hands on Nix's
shoulders, holding her at a distance as if seeing her for the
first time. I feel like we really turned a corner tonight, she
said. Then she disappeared into the elevator.

Nix rushed into the subway with her thoughts racing.
She was in it now. Really turned a corner? If only she knew,
what would I be to her then? And that house? More like a
mother trap. I can already feel the strings tugging. The
dinners, the random drop-ins, the extra set of keys. Zero
privacy. Constant supervision. I'd go insane in a month. I
escaped once, I'll be damned if I walk back into it now.

A couple transfers and a near mugging later, Nix
stepped out of the subway in her neighborhood of Little
Something-or-other. The rent was absurdly low, the crime
rate sky high. The price of living the artist's life in New York
City. Half the day was spent navigating the subway, the rest
finding excuses to delay heading home. Her mother never
got around to sending money. The college's financial aid
package only stretched so far. A roach infested studio in the

middle of the sticks was literally the best she could do. Before she met my father, most meals consisted of a baguette paired with one food group or another. Two were too much to swing at once. She weighed the situation against the promise of a lawn. Quiet tree-lined streets. Security. That's what really bugged her. She could stand living in exile as long as it was on her own terms. But there was a fraction of her that wanted domestic bliss. Questioned the merits of freedom, expression, fame. She fought tooth and nail to get out of that north Florida town. But now that she'd spent the better part of a year living on a block reeking of dogshit and curry, her idealistic visions of the city had dulled somewhat. She skidded past a group of teenagers with her eyes firmly planted on the sidewalk ahead and at last reached her graffitied front door. With practiced speed she unlocked it and slipped inside. Her mailbox was empty except for the usual bills. She climbed the four flights, dumped everything by the front door and beelined for the phone. She prayed my father would answer. It was supposed to be a night dedicated to his latest studio assignment. She went to hang up after a few rings but heard him cough roughly.

Hey, it's me, she said. You still working?

What? No. I was taking a nap.

So dedicated, she smiled, doing her best to keep the tone light.

Oh that? Yeah, I finished that a couple hours ago.

Didn't you start it a couple hours ago?

It's done. It's a masterpiece.

I'm sure. So if you're not working...

I'll be over in a few. You eat yet?

Not really. I mean, my mom and I went somewhere but she was watching everything I ate as if she could hear me getting fatter.

You're not fat.

You're sweet.

I'll pick something up. She heard the receiver click. She liked that they never said goodbye. It was as if they had their own little world that never stopped or restarted. They just were.

His cab pulled up as she got out of the shower. She threw on the first clothes she could find while he climbed the four flights up. He arrived on her landing with a few trays of sushi on one arm and a bucket of KFC on the other. Didn't know what you'd be in the mood for, he said. I love you, she answered. They stuck the California rolls in the fridge and chowed down on thick crispy drumsticks, sitting with their legs linked on the floor and discussing the dinner from hell.

Sounds to me, he said finally, Like your mom's on a whole other planet. You ever tried leveling with her?

Nix shook her head. She always assumes the worst anyways. Nothing I say makes the slightest difference.

He rose to trash the finished tub of chicken but stopped short. You tell her my name yet?

No, why?

Because, he said, chucking it in, I think I have a solution.

Honestly, I don't –

I think, he continued, we need to take her out tomorrow night and get her blitzed. I mean beyond drunk. Tell her story after story about us. The drugs, the sex, the murderous rampages, all under a fake name and all

111

designed to satisfy her worst fears. Then, when she's absolutely drunk herself into submission, we introduce her to the real me and tell her the truth. Not nearly so horrible by comparison. Thoughts?

I could imagine one or two things going wrong.

That's not so bad.

I'm being polite.

Your whole life your mother's been like this, right?

Yeah, but it's not as if she does it intentionally.

Isn't there even a small part of you that wants to mess with her?

Nix lay awake thinking over his proposition. He insisted she take the night before making a decision. By three o' clock she said Fuck it. She told him over breakfast the next morning and they renamed my father Jughead.

Nix and Jughead stopped by the farmer's market in Union Square after class. They figured a home-cooked meal was another way to stick it to the Queen of TV dinners. Jughead spared no expense. Two loaves ciabatta, truffle oil, olive oil, balsamic vinegar, rosemary, garlic, imported chilis. Fresh tomatoes, greens, peppers. Three kinds of cheese. Sausage. Homemade tartalle. A feast simple to prepare but nonetheless one she'd remember. The only hang-up came at the apple cart. Nix dedicated some granny smiths to bake a tart for dessert, but by the time she'd counted out the change Jughead had already bit into one. When she scolded him he playfully bit into a second. Nix cursed him out with a crowd watching and stalked off. He followed her to a stoop one block north where she fitfully talked through her anxiety about the dinner that night. At a loss for what else to say, Jughead attempted a few crude jokes at her mother's expense. They fell flat and the tears turned to fury. Nix shoved the groceries to the ground, called the night off, and headed for the subway. At the turnstile she realized she was too broke to even afford a token. The sobs came stronger than ever and she collapsed against the wall of the station. Someone tapped her shoulder. Suddenly she smelled the musk of urine and alcohol. Opening her eyes she saw a homeless man crouched down to face her, offering the coins she needed. When she noticed the duct tape in his hair the absurdity of everything hit her and she started laughing uncontrollably. The man smiled unsurely in turn, the gap in his teeth only sending her into louder fits. Her ribs ached she laughed so hard. Finally managing a No thank you she launched up the steps and back to the stoop. He was nowhere to be found. She circled the block before ending up in the market again, where she found him at the apple cart buying a dozen more apples, carrying the load of groceries she'd knocked to the ground.

Seeing her, he said, Now there's enough for both of us, Crazy.

She kissed him and hung around his neck. Thanks for putting up with me.

Thanks for the excellent sex.

Before they took off she led him on another tour of the food stalls, collecting bread, water, fruit, granola, and several homemade pastries. With the fresh collection in tow they headed down to the subway and delivered the spoils to the homeless man. Then they exited the station and caught a cab back to the apartment.

Her mother was an hour late. Despite Nix walking her through the directions twice. They waited at the window before finally getting a frantic call from a payphone in the Bronx. After a couple aborted attempts to learn her location

Jughead took the phone and talked the driver through how to reach the apartment. When her car at last arrived she leapt out the cab before it had fully stopped, leveled Nix with her eyes and barked, I don't know why you can't live in a nice neighborhood. Nix took her upstairs while Jughead settled the astronomical cab fare.

It proved difficult to reheat the dinner. The gas in the oven had cut out while they waited out front and the plates had cooled to room temperature. Just serve it as is, her mother snapped. No one's expecting a revelation. Turning to Jughead, she asked, Why in the Hell would your parents saddle you with a name like that?

They were cowpokes actually, he replied. They grew up down the same dirt road from one another. Sort of like brother and sister. Archie comics were the foundation of their home-schooling. It took until they were fifteen to finally consummate the romance. So when I popped out it was a natural fit.

Where'd they get the money to send you here?

They struck oil. We've been rolling in it every since. I occasionally sell methamphetamines to the kids at school, but that's not for the financial gain. More for the spiritual fulfillment it provides.

Nix set everyone's plates in front of them. Can I pour you some wine, Mom?

Her mother stared at her coldly, then turned back to Jughead. You're a piece of work, you know that? My daughter moves all the way to the big city convinced things are going to be different –

Mom –

Swearing she's better than everyone else –

Would you give me your glass?

Then she ends up falling for the same smart-ass son-of-a-bitch she could've found at home.

I'm not that smart, Jughead butted in. I'm an artist. And I eat a lot of paint. They're starting to affect my vision. You're a complete blur right now.

Turning to Nix, she asked, Is he this obnoxious all the time or did you put him up to it just to torture me?

Nix finished pouring her mother's wine and downed half the glass herself. With a crude smile she answered, Just to torture you of course. But you should really try his meth. Completely lucid high. Everyone ready for cold pasta?

Her mother rose. Where is the nearest subway?

Nix jumped out of her seat, knocking over everyone's wine glasses. You just got here!

I'm not staying for this.

You can't go Mom, you'll get lost.

Hey, babe? Jughead interjected, motioning to the puddle spreading across the floor.

So clean it up! she shouted back. Her mother was already out the door.

We were only having some fun, Jughead called after.

You're not helping, Nix hissed back. Her mother was a flight down and showed no sign of stopping. She took the steps two at a time in pursuit. Her voice echoed through the stairwell. When she caught up she had to fight to stay alongside. You can't go, okay? It's not safe.

If you can do it, so can I.

No you can't, you'll get raped.

I will not get raped.

Yes, you will, Mom!

I'll break it up if she gets raped, Jughead called.

They reached the ground floor. Nix pulled back her mother's shoulder but it did nothing to slow her down. Look, I'm sorry! she pleaded. Just come back? We're both really –

She had an abortion.

Her mother paused with her hand on the exit. Suddenly pale, visibly shaking, she turned to face her daughter. Nix tried to manage an apology but no sound came out. Jughead's shout from above had silenced them both. They just stood there trembling.

Jughead's heavy footsteps hit the landing one floor up. You guys there?

It occurred to Nix it was the most honest moment they'd ever had. Then her mother drew in, wound back, and struck her. Without a word she whipped open the door and left.

Nix barely noticed Jughead check her, rush outside, and return shaking his head. The cab driver was still out there, he said. She jumped in and they sped off. I knocked on the window but she wouldn't look at me.

She lost her legs and sat on the bottom step. He joined her. They stared at the trash pile. A pair of flies circled them. The heat in the hallway was stifling. She thought back to her meals that week. Tried to figure out if it was her garbage that smelled so bad. If it was her fault the world had gone to shit. Somewhere upstairs a baby cried its lungs out. A fresh wave of guilt hit her. The block in her throat burst open but she choked it back. The last thing she wanted was to collapse sobbing in his arms. When she recovered her breath she asked him a question. He didn't hear. Mustering her courage, she repeated, Why did you say that?

He stiffened up. I thought you wanted to be honest with her.

CONCRETE FEVER

Nix kept staring forward.

Are you actually blaming me for that? There was no way I could've known she'd react like... We planned on telling her. It's not my fault.

She stood and said, I'm going upstairs.

What do you want me to do, apologize for her overreacting?

She fingered the keys in her pocket and started climbing.

What do you want me to do?

She kept going, not caring if he stayed or left.

***

The class loved Jughead's latest work. Nix found herself at a loss. It's just the same old shit, she said under her breath. Meanwhile her own piece was a mess. She realized as much. An overabundance of images, a complete lack of direction. She wanted to torch the thing. Only the firecode stopped her. The professor mentioned it twice during his first day's introduction to the class. Apparently students at their school had a predisposition toward fire.

She grabbed her bag and cut out early. She doubted anyone would notice, least of all Jughead. In her pocket she found some of his crumpled bills leftover from the market and decided to spend them. She wandered aimlessly for a while before ending up at a movie theater. She paid admission to a film she had no intention of seeing, headed for the refreshment counter, bought a large tub of popcorn, and left the building. She ate her way to the bottom in the courtyard of St. Mark's Church. When she couldn't stomach the last bites she left them for a sleeping homeless man.

She walked through nightfall. The world felt contaminated with people. She wished she could find some open space. She missed Mexico. She missed the feeling of possibility. She missed knowing what she wanted. Her mother wouldn't answer her phone calls. Now that the offer was off the table, she found herself imagining a little house of her own. The idea no longer sent chills down her spine. In her head she planted an herb garden, named three cats, designed a color scheme for the kitchen. As her artwork became less and less inspired, more and more she craved a new direction forward.

Without warning she got sick outside a bodega. The owner was nice enough. Happened a dozen times a week in that neighborhood. Too much sun, Nix determined. She got onto the subway looking forward to a quiet night at home. Chinese delivery. A hot bath. Maybe work if she was up to it. No pressure. If the mood didn't strike there was no need to force it.

Jughead was waiting outside her building when she arrived. About time, he called. You had me waiting so long I nearly had to make it with a guy named Gonzalo. In his hands he held a couple trays of sushi.

She walked past him to the entrance. She unlocked it and ducked inside, not bothering to hold open the door. He threw his foot forward just in time and followed her up the stairs.

Did I do something wrong? he asked.

What makes you say that? she said, not looking back.

Because you're acting weird.

Sounds like my problem then.

You can talk to me, you know.

Who said there's anything to talk about?

CONCRETE FEVER

Is this how it's going to be all night?

You're the one who invited himself over.

He stopped her on the next landing. In the apartment beside them a baby was crying.

Would you mind? she said, trying to pull away.

Not until you talk to me.

We're almost at my apartment. Can we just –

No. Now.

The baby cried louder. Nix really couldn't stand listening to it. I'm feeling sick, okay?

Sick.

Yes.

Is that why you left class early?

I didn't think you noticed.

Of course I did.

You didn't follow.

Was I supposed to? It seemed pretty obvious you –

She shoved away his hand and continued up the stairs. Once inside, she busied herself getting settled, pretending not to notice him brooding by the door. A full five minutes passed without a word. Suddenly she felt nauseous again and sat down. He went and poured her a glass of water.

You never have any ice, he called from the freezer.

Sue me, she said, covering her eyes.

He brought over the glass and she drank it down. When she finished he went and got her another. She hesitated, unable to stomach any more. He took her glass, set it down, and returned to his perch by the door. Then all they could do was look at one another, trying to find the right words. At last she closed her eyes again, head resting against the back of the futon couch they'd found on a street corner in the Village. Suddenly, she felt the cushion sag to her right and his fingers combing back the hair from her forehead. For the moment she was at peace.

Your painting's a piece of shit, he said gently.

I know, she said.

What do you think it is?

I don't know. Maybe I'm not meant to –

Don't be stupid, he interrupted. You're the most original in the department.

Don't lie to me, she said softly.

I'm not.

Original is one of those words people use when they don't have anything to say. Like interesting, or eclectic. If I hear one more person use the word visceral...

Well I don't know how else to put it. Everybody knows how good you are. Lately you're just trying too hard.

She got up and went into the bathroom, leaving the door open. He heard the faucet running and followed. She stood there throwing handfuls of water on her face and rubbing it over the back of her neck. Seeing him in the mirror she paused. Turned off the faucet. Without facing him she asked, What do you want me to say? You're better than I am.

I am not.

Don't lie, she said again, brushing past. She continued out of sight into the bedroom.

I'm not, he called after her. Looking in he saw her pulling off her clothes, drenched and sticking to her body after a day in the sun. She noticed him staring and swung the door closed. When she opened it again he was gone.

Nix and Jughead never officially called it off. They still exchanged looks across the classroom. To make him jealous she went out with one of the other students. The effort backfired. The guy had severe personal hygiene problems. He took her to a friend's play and she spent the whole of the first act pinching her nose. At intermission she said she felt sick and left. After that she simply retreated each night to her apartment for a renewed life of poverty.

Nix was pregnant a second time. She suspected it for weeks before she managed the courage to take a test. She took another just to be sure. There was no question. She was bringing a bastard into the world.

She made a promise to herself the last time: if it ever happened again, she'd keep it. The details from the visit wouldn't disappear. The sidelong glances entering the building. The nonchalant receptionist. The ice cold operating table. She had dreams that haunted her. She was consumed by guilt she barely understood. Her family's brief bout of church-going wasn't the reason. Part of it was her mother's silence. She started to think it was the fact she'd chosen one path over another, presumably her true destiny, but recently she'd lost faith. She couldn't make art the way she used to, and that was the whole reason she went through with it in the first place. Now she was lost. She missed Jughead like crazy. She refused to call him. He knew nothing of her condition. She had no idea how many months along she was. She simply trudged through her days, commuting between boroughs, throwing up as necessary. She had no friends. No family she could talk to. She had unwittingly made him the center of her world. She doubted he ever did the same.

Then came the day when she puked on her canvas. The whole class watched on, mildly surprised. Half of them figured it was a new medium she was working with. The professor offered to help but Jughead was already guiding her to fresh air. Outside, he got the truth. Within two weeks he accepted a job offer on Wall Street and dropped out of art school to start a family.

***

Naturally, Jughead got the position through his family's contacts. He didn't tell them the reason he wanted the job. All he said was that he'd lost interest in the whole art thing and hoped to dedicate his time to something worthwhile. His family was overjoyed. Bought him a full wardrobe of designer suits. Paid for a cropped haircut. Passed on the family watch. His father educated him in workplace etiquette. Eventually he would try to do the same for me. I would prove much less receptive.

Nix worried the father of her child was turning into a robot. She brought it up one day. The next afternoon he showed up with a jagged heart tattooed on his chest. Same color tone, same slash pattern as the marks of her scar. Should stay out of sight, he said, and this way I remember who I'm doing it for.

The night before his first day, they stayed up all hours. Philosophical conversation. Raids on the fridge. A trip or two to bed. It was their way of letting go. Dawn cracked and the alarm rang out. He rose out of bed a zombie. Nix was nowhere to be found. Jughead lost his motivation. Nearly called the whole thing quits. Then she returned holding an iced coffee and egg sandwich for him. She handed them over beaming with pride. He promised he wouldn't let her down. She kissed him and went to start his shower. It always took a while for the hot water to kick in.

In studio, Jughead could do no wrong. Every sketch was inspired, every painting was a masterpiece. The business world proved no different. He won notice immediately for his quiet self-confidence, his irreverent humor, his obvious intelligence. No one suspected he wasn't old enough to drink. Thanks to his family's reputation he was given responsibilities far beyond his pay grade with the intention of moving him up the ladder quickly. He took drinks at lunch with his superiors and they returned clapping each other on the back. Laughing as they settled back behind their desks.

Then came the realization he would have never expected: he was actually good at his job. He never cared much for art, if he was honest with himself. Success had always come too easily. Most of the appeal had to do with the lifestyle. Growing his hair down to his shoulders. Smoking against buildings. Making cynical remarks. The attention he got was definitely a selling point. But at the firm he discovered a new high. And like any drug, the pride of accomplishment slowly took hold.

Nix was on the periphery. She saw him less and less. The first trimester he was home every night by six. With two months to go she was lucky if she saw him before ten. She routinely smelled drinks on his breath. He never pretended otherwise. He was drinking with the higher ups, working the system. It was how the company ran. If he wasn't moving up, he was moving down. He was doing it for all of them, he said, hand on her stomach. He won her over but she missed him like crazy. Days in the apartment passed like a prison sentence. The doctor put her on bedrest. She moved into Jughead's apartment, unofficially. The lease on her own place stayed active. Rather than face her landlady she had him pay the rent each month until the lease expired. Chump change now that he was building his own stash. They hadn't

Nathaniel Kressen

taken money from his family in months. Nonetheless, they insisted on sending things the baby. All of them hideous. Nix gagged at the sight of the pale pink crib. It sat at the edge of the bed. Right past her swelling feet.

Jughead came home one day to find her standing at her canvas, affixing torn bits of baby clothing to a sloppy mess of acrilycs, paste, and paperclips. What are you doing?

It's going to be a boy, she said, eyes on the canvas. All the crap your family bought is pink.

The doctor said...

I don't care what the doctor said, I know my body.

That's not what I... You're supposed to be lying down.

And you're supposed to be taking care of me.

Where do you think I am all day?

Please, you enjoy it.

I make peace with it. We don't have another option, we need the money... You want to stop that and look at me?

She did, nonetheless refusing to sit. You could come home afterwards.

We already discussed this.

Well, we're discussing it again. I can't go outside. I'm a beached whale in here.

It won't be forever.

Well until it changes I'd appreciate some company.

He turned away and said under his breath, And I'd like some peace and quiet.

What was that?

Nothing.

What did you say?

Why don't you lie down like you're supposed to and I'll order us dinner.

I'm sick of ordering in.

CONCRETE FEVER

Are you going to cook? Because I'm spent.

And drunk.

I didn't even go out today, I was at the office until, what, 45 minutes ago? I came straight home. Just like you wanted.

Why didn't you say that then?

Because you blew up at me the second I came in the door.

No. First, you criticized me.

You're supposed to be on bedrest.

The doctor doesn't know what he's talking about.

Jughead slammed the closet door shut. Do you want me to go back out? Because that's what you're driving toward.

Nix studied him. Where did that come from?

I work all day, and this is what I come home to?

Excuse me?

Forget it.

No, I want to know what's so horrible about coming home.

... You get upset at me no matter what I do. There's always something. Me going out when I'm trying to get promoted. Me working Saturdays when we need the money. And if it's not the job then it's the marriage thing. It's like static in my head. Of course I'm going to drink.

The marriage thing. Nice. Really romantic.

It is a thing at this point. It's just an institution. You know how I feel about you.

Yeah, apparently I'm drag to come home to. She headed for the door.

Where are you going?

Out.

No you're not.

Try and stop me.

He blocked the doorway. She pushed him full force, bore knuckles into his ribs, pinched his stomach. Nothing worked. Finally she threw her bag down and slowly lowered herself into a chair. She tried not to show how exhausted she felt.

A silence fell. When he spoke again his tone had softened. I'd marry you tomorrow if that's what you wanted.

Okay. I want it.

Okay then.

Tomorrow?

I'll have to find you a wheelchair, make it down to City Hall. And I'll have to clear the day off with work.

She fixed him with her eyes, letting him know the stakes. He understood. By the next night they were married, having scheduled an impromptu service with a couple art school friends as witnesses. None of their parents attended.

The legal attachment did little to change things. Nix still felt abandoned. Jughead still drank. When she went into labor no one could locate him. I was delivered nine pm on a Tuesday, my mother crying loudly and my father on a bender. The next morning he finally arrived. He took me in his arms, and a brief, wondrous moment took place. Promises were made, resolutions adopted. The past months faded. The clarity seemed endless. Our family became sober, healthy, and happy.

CONCRETE FEVER

Nathaniel Kressen

Gypsy pulled on her coat. Went to the door. Held it open expectantly. I hesitated. I'd suggested the destination. I needed answers. Nevertheless, I couldn't shake the feeling that leaving the apartment was a risk. We'd found a sense of security there, established our own rhythm. The outside world threatened to shove me back into the same dark place I'd been my whole life. Wouldn't take much. I weighed the letters in my hand. With a sinking stomach, I realized there was no way I could let them slide until morning. I secured the flask in my jacket pocket. Thought about our twin chemical stashes. They'd keep us running a while yet. I zipped my coat shut. Looked to Gypsy. Hungry smile on her lips. I grabbed my keys and walked with her to the elevator. It hadn't left since we got there. We piled in and headed down, once again stopping floor by floor.

Looks like the pills did the trick, she said between spit takes, motioning to my ankle.

I rotated it a couple times, shifted it side to side. Sure enough, the pain was gone.

I stumbled out of the building expecting the city in ruins. Not sure why. Late hour maybe. The letters. The pills. The streets were packed though. Gypsy bounded ahead to talk to the homeless man she'd been staring at. Turned out to be a woman with whiskers and she came back sprinting. Some guy yelled behind us. Gypsy took my arm. He yelled again. I turned to look but she jerked me forward. I lost my balance. She sped ahead. The guy streaked past me and the two of them disappeared around a corner.

I found them half a block away, pressed against each other under a scaffolding. Rough but familiar. I limped closer and heard him barking.

You want to tell me how he got my address?! The cops showed up. They threatened me with statutory. You want that on my record heading into law school?

When I got there I stood tall as I could, the ankle buckling under. There a problem?

He stared at me a second, then said, She wrap you up in this too?

She tried to move but he grabbed hold of her arm. The street went red. I forced a step forward. Get your hand off her.

He looked down at me and laughed. You gotta be kidding me.

Now.

Trust me, guy, you have no idea who this girl is.

Get. Your hand. Off.

He cracked his back and sighed heavy. I looked him over. A good three inches taller, an extra thirty pounds of muscle. Still, you could see weakness in his eyes. You could always spot transplants to the city. I laughed, picturing his mother paying his rent. Gypsy's diagnosis came back to me.

CONCRETE FEVER

Here was the suburban jerkoff she pegged me for. He shifted, realizing there was no way I was moving. What are you going to do, hit me? he asked. You look beat to hell already.

I rolled my sleeves. Gypsy caught my eye and mouthed, Just go, okay? Then she dug her head into her coat. A kitten slowly getting crushed.

He sidled up to me as if we were friends. What are you, twelve?

Sure, I'm twelve.

Look, she's really not worth it. She's hot as anything, believe me, I know. But she's categorically insane. Her dad's apparently been calling her all night cause she snuck out. Now he's sending cops to my place. Plus she stole a bunch of my stuff and won't tell me what she did with it. Just grabbed a bag full and ran –

Up the fire escape?

His eyes flickered. He stepped into me, forcing me back onto the bad ankle. It buckled and I hurried to right myself. He kept coming. How'd you know that?

Doesn't matter, I said. It's trashed. All of it. Hope there wasn't anything mommy can't buy you again.

I hit the ground, and only then felt where his fist had connected. I forced an eye open. He was back squeezing her arm. It looked ready to snap. I heard their voices but couldn't make out the words. She looked scared for her life. That's all I understood for sure.

I remembered that schoolyard fight. I lost all logic to prove a point. Took punch after punch. Bled out. Scarred up. Broke apart. Stole whatever breaths I could. That kid should have taken me apart. He didn't. I had too much at stake to stay down. I swore then I'd always stick up for myself. In

131

Nathaniel Kressen

time the promise faded. My reputation didn't matter. I never had any pride. I lost the ability to empathize, so there was nobody to defend. Far as I was concerned, there was nothing worth fighting for. Then I heard Gypsy cry out, and all that changed. I was on my feet before I knew it.

I pushed him back into the crossbar of the scaffold. His spine inverted and he grabbed hold of my collar to right himself. We tugged at one another for an advantage. At a loss for what else to do, I headbutted him and sent us both into shock, grabbing our foreheads to stop the tremors running through. Not sure what I'd expected to happen. I watched a lot of pro wrestling as a kid.

Before I'd got the blur from my eyes he pushed me flush against one of the brick posts of the stoop entrance. He threw his fist into my stomach with surprising force. Knocked the wind out of me. I tightened my abs and tried to force the air back in. Same as the rooftop. Only a game. Within my control. But it wasn't. He righted me and shot another punch into my stomach. I collapsed but he caught me. Threw another. And another. And another.

I fell to my hands and knees, panting. Out of the corner of my eye I saw him easing away from me, stalking toward Gypsy. I kicked out blindly and somehow managed to catch the back of his knee. He dropped hard, hitting his kneecap on the concrete. I took a shallow breath and went to take advantage. I limped over and swung hard as I could at the side of his head. The punch landed just above his ear. I didn't see how he took it. Despite Gypsy's drugs the pain in my hand shot back like wildfire and I froze where I stood, clenching it to my stomach. Little damage done, the fucker rose and drove me back into the steps. I landed awkwardly, vertebrae stretched across jagged edges and cracking in succession. He brought his weak hand to my hair and pulled a fistful. Then he rained punch after punch down on my face. I didn't feel much after the first two. Only a warmth spreading from the bridge of my nose on down. My eyes went wet. The street behind him went blacker with each hit. I couldn't get my arms to move. They just hung limp at my sides while he lent his full force to fucking me up. I gave up trying to fight him off. He kept right on going. I wondered if I'd fooled myself, if I weren't still drunk in the stairwell, or up on the rooftop even. When the hits finally stopped I couldn't see anything. His weight lifted off and moved to parts unknown. To my satisfaction, I felt no pain. I smiled up at where I guessed he might be standing. I tasted blood in my mouth and thought of Gypsy with ketchup on her teeth. Instantly I fought to regain my senses. I couldn't let him hurt her. I blinked rapidly, shocks of electricity shooting through my head. I slowly distinguished a streetlight and summoned the strength to move toward it. Rediscovered my limps and forced them into action. Rose to my feet. Swaying where I stood, the rest came into focus. My new friend was staring at me, Gypsy a few feet past him.

Thah awl yew gawh, fffucker? I slurred, blood spilling out of my mouth.

His eyes shifted from me to her and back again, then to the red mess on his hands. He passed Gypsy without a word. I felt a surge of pride seeing that I'd taken out his knee. He grabbed onto the bar of the scaffold for support, then transferred with difficulty to the entry gates opposite. When even those left him he hopped one-footed, bracing himself on a slick building façade until he disappeared out of sight.

Gypsy rushed to me. In my new muddled language I told her I was fine. She made me sit anyway. The exhaustion

Nathaniel Kressen

hit me full force. She had me pinch my nose. I could already feel it swelling. Then she ran to get ice from an all night deli. I waited, splayed out on the sidewalk. I didn't mind the damage done. I got what I fought for.

She held it herself against my face. Time passed. Softly she asked, You do that for me?

I shifted so my mouth wasn't covered. Swung my tongue around my mouth and overenunciated each word. Ending up speaking clearer than either of us expected. I said, Don't ask stupid questions.

Is it stupid because it's yes or stupid because it's no?

Pretty obvious.

Say it anyway.

... Stupid because it's no. I'm a masochist. More pain the better. Look at me.

You do look pathetic.

Would've been worse if I jumped.

Quicker though. Painless maybe.

Not that bad now.

She scoffed. Guys can never admit when they're hurt.

I can. This isn't bad.

Oh yeah? Try sitting up straight.

I shifted. My body shrieked in five different places. I laid back again. Don't want to right now, I said.

Right, she replied.

... If I'd jumped we never would have had dinner.

Or followed the moon.

Seen that band.

Found the nexus of the universe.

Gone back to my place.

... We wouldn't have done a lot of things. She peeled the ice pack off me. The traffic amplified. She poured the excess

134

water from the bag. It found the cracks in the sidewalk and slowly drained toward the gutter. A cab appeared. I tried to call it but my arm wouldn't move. It sped past. I could only imagine how we looked. There was no one but Gypsy to gauge by.

So, about my dad…

I shook my head.

Don't you want to hear the truth?

We had an agreement. Nuff said.

And now?

Now, I don't know.

But you got your ass kicked for me.

Well don't put it like that.

How should I?

I fought for you. Emphasize the effort, not the outcome.

Either way, I feel like I owe you an explanation.

You know why I fought that guy?

Why?

… Forget it. Tonight's just a game. It doesn't mean anything.

She laid her head on my shoulder. Probably the one part of me that wasn't sore. We breathed there for a while, our bruises darkening together. She peeled back her skirt to the point where I could see the pale of her upper thigh, and the series of slash marks there. I hadn't noticed them in the stairwell. Some were recent, others older. Fading scars against fresh wounds. She picked a scab. It broke off. When she started talking I couldn't stop her.

Sometimes I lose track of what's real and what's made up. If I actually drowned in the Hudson or if it was a dream. If this city is just some purgatory. Most of the time I feel like I'm on this train off its rails, speeding a hundred miles an hour without knowing where I'm going. Scared I'm going to die any second. Scared I'm already dead. Used to be only some days I felt like that... I don't know if I'd ever jump. Seems way too final. All I need is silence every now and then. Things to be simple.

She lit a couple cigarettes. She placed one in my mouth and it stuck against my lips.

I don't know what's up with my dad. I get these dreams of dark dark shit happening between him and me when I was a kid, and literally have no idea if my mind invented it or not. He's alright most of the time, just... I kind of feel exposed with you not talking.

What do you want me to say?

Something. Anything. That you're not going to like, run away.

I can't run.

You know what I mean.

We locked eyes. For a moment it seemed like we might kiss. Then the moment passed. I focused on the cigarette. The ash burned the open sores in my mouth. The night swelled a moment, then atrophied as I exhaled. I half-wanted the night to be over. I had enough wounds. Still, my chest sunk when I thought of leaving.

My dad did die in the towers, I said. I wasn't lying about that.

I didn't think you were, she said.

... You want to tell me why you're doing this?

Doing what?

This.

Why are you?

The other choice was the sidewalk. And I'm a coward.

I don't think that.

Come on.

I don't know. To find out if magic exists, I guess. Same as you.

Pretty messed up way of doing it.

Um, I don't know if you've looked at us lately, but we kind of fit the description.

I turned my head to spit. It came out a black mass of tar and blood.

See? she laughed.

All at once I realized I was shivering. I pictured steam rising from the rips in my skin. The life leaving me one breath at a time. The vacant street became a freezer. The buildings warped. The streetlights circled me on all sides and stretched out of sight over the scaffolding. I was nothing but a corpse awaiting burial. Then she placed her palm on my face. Its warmth spidered through me and the world, just for a moment, evened out.

***

I watched the water miles below as we sped out of Manhattan. Vaguely considered what would have happened had I chosen a bridge instead of a rooftop. I glanced back at Gypsy. Her hair tumbled from the open window and she fought to fix it. I reached over and pulled her hands away. I liked it messed up.

Our taxi eased off the bridge and into the borough. The avenues widened. The streetlights dimmed. The pot holes sabotaged us. We lurched through nondescript project housing. Blurred past darkened townhouses. Paused in front of the public high school where kids from my former neighborhood went. I couldn't vouch for the education they

137

got, but the basketball rims were bent to hell and the court had ditches every few feet. Puddles shone red from the stoplight. They'd turn to ice by morning.

We pulled up to my old building a few blocks away, a dilapidated two-family stuck between new developments. The divorce gave my mother enough for a downpayment back when the area was nothing but a place to get shot. The ground floor was rented out. She lived in the basement with a separate entrance in back. As I opened the gate Gypsy squeezed my wrist. I nodded to reassure her and locked back up. I led her past a series of vacant windows to the backyard, strewn with abandoned sculpture projects and piles of dead sod.

What are you going to say to her? she asked. I felt for the letters in my coat. Still there. I took a breath and keyed open the door.

As usual, the heat was on full blast. I barely noticed anymore but one look at Gypsy reminded me. It's a sauna in here, she whispered.

She does everything overkill. In winter it's the heat, in summer it's the AC.

Gypsy's eyes widened. Is that her?

I squinted. The lights were off but there was enough blue from the television to see a figure laid out on the couch. I spotted an overturned wine glass and melted tub of ice cream on the floor. Yeah that's her.

She passed out?

That's where she always sleeps. I had the one bedroom.

That was nice of her.

Sure, I said. You try going through puberty with only a piece of plywood separating you from your mother. She has horrible ears though. A war could roll through here and she'd go right on sleeping.

I walked over to the bathroom, switched on the light, and got a shock looking in the mirror. Turned on the faucet and threw handfuls of water on my face. Pried the crusted blood from under my nose. I searched for some hydrogen peroxide or Neosporin. All I found were antidepressants. Until then I'd half-forgotten why I came. The familiarity of being home again erased my agenda for the visit. For a minute I considered pouring her pills down the drain. I reached for a towel and glimpsed the end of Gypsy's skirt passing out of sight.

I found her standing in the doorway to my bedroom. For a while we just stared, the objects gradually coming into focus. Baseball pennants on the wall. Stuffed animals on the dresser. An ancient pair of pajama bottoms in the corner.

My face went hot. I wanted to torch everything. I never brought anyone there, so I never bothered getting rid of my childhood possessions. I'd tell people we couldn't go because of the area. A health food grocery and handful of bars didn't change the fact that it was an armpit of a neighborhood. Really, it was because of my mom. The one time I did bring a friend home he made fun of her the next day to our entire class. I had to blacken his eye just to get some peace. I fought the urge to check Gypsy's expression, instead circling the twin bed to throw everything in the closet.

When's the last time you were here? she asked.

Few months ago, I said. October probably.

Looks like you still know where everything is.

I should. Basically spent my whole life here.

After a minute I finished up and went to exit. She hugged me in the doorway. One of my ribs ached so I readjusted. She didn't let go. It's hard being back here, isn't it?

It's alright.

You don't have to act strong.

I'm not.

Just know you don't have to.

I eased out of her grip, crossed the room and flicked on the overhead. We hardly ever used it because the light was stale somehow and made you feel sick. There were only slits for windows so no daylight got in. The floor was perpetually covered in junk. The shag carpet reeked from the rain getting in. I moved some folded laundry from a chair so Gypsy could sit. Then I pushed aside some chinese food containers and sat on the coffee table.

Hey Nix. Wake up.

Nix? Gypsy asked.

She never answers to Mom when I try to wake her up. I placed a hand on her shoulder and rocked until her eyes opened. Hey Mom, happy to see me? She stared vacant for a few seconds, then bee-lined for the bathroom and puked into the sink. The door stayed open and we heard every last detail.

Don't be an alcoholic like your father, she said as I returned her to the couch.

You're the one throwing up.

Something I ate.

You want water?

Her head had already fallen back.

Hey!

Her eyes spun around the room before settling on me.

I'm here to talk to you.

She clacked her lips. They'd gone white from the heat.

I'm going to get you some water. You going to stay awake?

Mmm.

The kitchen was open to the rest of the room, making it all too easy for the mess to spill in. It took effort to find a clean glass, and a good minute to clear space in the sink to fill it. I didn't bother checking for ice. I was the one who filled the tray. When I got back she was staring unapologetically at Gypsy, who looked pretty on edge.

Who's this? she asked.

A friend.

Your friend have a naaaame? She was getting sloppier by the second.

She's my guardian angel. What's it matter, Mom? I handed her the glass and made her drink. I mouthed an apology to Gypsy.

I don't do parents, she said.

This won't take long. I pulled off my coat and took out the letters. Sat back down on the table and took her glass from her hand. What are these?

Her eyes narrowed, forehead scrunching. Finally she said, Letters.

I know they're letters. You see the address?

I can't see, honey.

Then open your eyes.

There's no reason to yell. What time is it?

It's our address. They're addressed to me.

That's good. Good to have friends.

They're from dad.

... Your father's dead, sweetheart.

He's been sending them since I was ten.

Her eyes closed.

Are you even listening to me?

Yes, honey.

Hey! I snapped my fingers in her face. Her eyes shot open. For a moment she was alert.

What happened to your face?

That doesn't matter, Mom.

Let me get you some...

You don't have any ice. What I need from you is -

I'll go get some. Where are my keys?

I'm fine, okay? I'm alright. I need you to focus on this.

On what?

The letters. From Dad. Why didn't I get these?

Because I had them returned, she said. He was terrible to us.

I stomached my anger and said, I don't remember him doing anything.

You were just a child.

I'm not now.

Yes you are.

Who are you kidding? I've been gone three months and look at yourself. I've always taken care of the both of us.

My mother's eyes hardened. Everyone's tired, she said. We'll call it a night and talk another time.

I'm not leaving here without an answer. You owe me that.

Another time, she said.

Gypsy tugged at the back of my shirt.

I want an answer now, I said, ignoring her.

CONCRETE FEVER

Gypsy pulled again, hard enough to get me up on my feet. She'd already grabbed my coat and was guiding us toward the door.

I shook her off and stayed my ground. Talk to me!

The answer is you're just a child, she answered. Your father and I were children.

And then you got petty and he got drunk, is that it?

Her jaw tightened, her wrinkles stretched. She looked ready to snap but maintained an even tone. Everything's black and white for you.

How could it not be? My whole life you told me he abandoned us, and then I find these?!

He did abandon us.

Then why won't you explain?

It doesn't matter what you found.

Of course it does!

You're a child. All you have are possibilities. Your father's money saw to that. Where was he when you were growing up? Same city. Where was he? It's always been the two of us. I'm sure I wasn't the greatest mother, honey, but at least...

You lied to me. These letters...

Are what? His confessions? His regrets? He had chances to fix whatever he wanted to. He's been writing those for years, he knew you weren't getting them. Being a father is one thing. Throwing money around is something else. One day, you'll have your chance to be an adult. To do better than either of us. And sweetheart, I pray you do. But until then you're just a spoiled, ungrateful child blaming what few problems you have on your parents' shortcomings.

Gypsy tugged again but the breath had left me.

Nathaniel Kressen

I don't doubt your father loved you. But he was sick. He couldn't help it.

How am I... supposed to...?

I don't know, sweetheart. Force yourself. Things might get better for you. They certainly never did for me.

Her face sagged, her energy spent, the drunk returning. With a sad smile she rose and walked past us to the bathroom. Before closing the door, she said, It's late. Sleep here if you want. I haven't touched your room since you left.

***

With no cabs around we headed for the subway, a good fifteen minute walk. The heat in the apartment made me sweat through the back of my shirt and the cold air gave me chills. By the time we hit the station I couldn't stop shaking.

It didn't prove much better underground. There was something unnerving about seeing an unmanned MTA booth at night that far into the boroughs. It seemed inevitable we were going to get mugged. Felt like entering some low-income graveyard where they can't get the grass to grow. Where the death's so real you can feel it. Stepping over the turnstile proved foolish. Felt my vertebrae shift like a California fault line. Gypsy went ahead, oblivious. An ice-cold drop of water smacked me square in the eye. I wiped it with a sleeve. The siren in my head wouldn't quit. I pulled out the flask and drank. Absently questioned how the hell I was still standing after all the punishment I'd got. The alcohol, the injuries, the mindfucks that just kept coming. I wondered if I'd ever hit a threshold that made me realize I actually wanted to live.

CONCRETE FEVER

We went to sit but suddenly heard a train approaching. Stunned, we boarded and took it toward Manhattan. Gypsy insisted we walk from car to car. It's amazing how something like a series of empty train cars seems beautiful in a city like New York. The only people we saw were a handful of drunks, lowlifes, and general undesirables. I liked thinking they were worse off than us. All the same it horrified me when I caught my reflection in the darkened train window. I averted my eyes and kept walking. In the next to last car we caught sight of a drunk college boy, passed out, destined for the end of the line. She wanted to take his wallet, I wouldn't let her. She drew a lipstick penis on his face instead and continued to the rear of the train.

We rode to the financial district, then got off to transfer. The train pulled out of sight. We walked toward an exit. Eyeing her, I thought she looked like one of those zombie chicks from the horror movies. Shadows falling vicious on her face, scary but sexy all the same. Each step shortened, each movement stunted. I opened my mouth to mention it but stopped. Seemed stupid to ask if she was tired.

We sat on the platform for the next train, legs dangling over the tracks.

You got street salt on your skirt, I managed at last.

She looked. Sure enough the colored patches were covered in a dull vomit gray. She reached in her bag, pulled out a switchblade, and ripped through the fabric from mid-thigh on down. Damn, she said. Looks like it's ripped now too.

I stared at the blade while she smiled expectantly. I looked away. The parallels to my mother were becoming a little unsettling. From the dark of the tunnel I heard

145

someone call me. I glanced back at Gypsy but realized she didn't know my real name. I concentrated on the dark. She asked what was up, I told her to be quiet. I listened with the intensity of a schizo. She tried talking and I threw a hand over her mouth.

She laughed, throwing it off. You're acting tough again.

No I'm not.

Aloof. Loofy. Loofa. I'm going to take a shower when we get back and scrub myself with you. Loofa... It wasn't that bad, you know. The way she tore into you. I know it probably sucked from your perspective, but honestly, it wasn't all that harsh.

I'm not looking for sympathy.

You're killing my buzz.

Dip into your stash.

I left it back at your place. But that's not what I was saying. I mean everything. Our night together. High in and of itself, don't you think?

The voice from the tunnel rose up again. Words too faint to make out. I leaned forward, nearly falling into the tracks.

I liked us talking before. In front of the stoop.

Do you hear that?

Hear what?

From the tunnel. That voice.

It's probably a radio or something.

I slid off the platform and onto the tracks.

She gagged. What are you doing?

I checked. Double-checked. No train in sight. I stepped over the first rail. The world didn't end so I kept walking toward the mouth of the tunnel. Gypsy screamed somewhere behind me. Terror in her voice. Didn't know she could get that loud. I paused at the arch. The voice ahead in the darkness. It dropped to a moan, then a whisper. I convinced myself it was my imagination. No way was I going forward. Then a wave of fury hit me. I saw my mother passed out, my father cut short, the footage of the towers on constant repeat. Of all things, I landed on Gypsy's freight train of an ex-boyfriend, looking at me like I wasn't worth the time it'd take to beat me with his fists. As I stared into the void, I realized he'd been right. I was ready to off myself hours ago, nothing had changed. I got laid, so what? It seemed different at the time, it wasn't. It was foolish to hope for anything more with Gypsy. She'd leave. Whatever truths I thought I'd found, they were fantasy. Fleeting. All the same, I was sick of things passing me by. I wanted to disappear down a hole and come out enlightened. I wanted something to justify not jumping.

Gypsy leapt on my shoulders from behind. Made my heart skip. Got you! she cheered. I sounded real right? Like I was actually scared? It's not that big a deal walking down here. Me and my friends from the orphanage used to do it all the time.

Another drop of water hit, this time finding my neck. It rolled down the back of my coat and I winced, throwing her off.

What is it? she asked.

Cold water hit me, I said disjointedly.

Watch it! She shot her hand forward and brought me against her. With the backlight from the platform I couldn't read her expression. Third rail, she said from the dark. You nearly touched it.

I looked around, noticing markers glowing, mapping everything out.

Don't you read the posters? It's like, instant death. What are we doing down here?

I heard something. A voice.

There's nobody down here, Jumper.

If you're afraid of getting caught you can turn back.

She laughed. Is that what you think? I'm just trying to get a read on you is all.

I felt her hand close over mine, then her lips on my cheek. Without a word she guided us forward. It wasn't long before I lost the impulse to check for trains. There were a number of inverted stoplights braced on the walls above us, all set to red. I figured there'd be some change before we needed to worry. The light was minimal, but with the rail markers it was enough to get by. It was how I'd imagine walking the tarmac at JFK.

We walked in silence. Occasionally we'd hear the scurrying of rats, or distant clanking sounds. Water dripping. Electricity surging on either side of us. Still, it was quiet enough to feel enveloped.

When I was twelve, my father dropped out of sight for a while. My mother signed me up for Boy Scouts to provide a male father figure for me to look up to. Instead I got a bunch of pseudo-outdoorsmen obsessed with their own kids. The only time I got their attention was when I did something wrong. Before long I lost interest and accepted falling through the cracks.

Must have gone on plenty of camping trips but only one sticks out in my mind. Winter trip upstate, snow-covered mountainside. Open-walled lean-tos for the adventurous, soaked bottom tents for the rest. I snuck off during dinner to jerk off in the woods. I'd recently discovered my body but had no one to explain it to me. The realities of cause and effect hadn't hit home yet, and after I'd pulled long enough it surprised me to explode. I soaked my hands clean in the snow, nearly getting frostbite in the process. An odd clarity took hold as I zipped myself back in. The distant laughter of the camp, the absolute darkness, the crisp air with only the faintest touch of wind. I lost track of where I ended and the world began. A feeling of love welled up in my chest. It seemed any second I'd achieve some epiphany to end the sadness that was already nagging at me.

Walking with Gypsy, swallowed in the tunnel, it seemed the answer might finally come. The darkness stifled reality. It was the surface of the moon. The depths of the ocean. A busted earth where we were lone survivors of the apocalypse. I smiled at the thought. Us responsible for repopulating the planet. What a problematic human race that would be.

Every now and then she would squeeze my hand. Felt good being reminded that she hadn't let go. It occurred to me we hadn't kissed since before the fight. I wondered if it was now off limits since we'd gone outrightly honest. Finally, she broke the silence. You still think I'm magic?

Is that a question, or a statement?

She didn't answer.

I decided to keep it light. I thought you were going to open your wings and fly away?

Later.

Why not now?

I don't know.

I think you do, I said without thinking. Heart on my sleeve. I cursed myself. It was a game, all of it, and I had to acknowledge that or risk... Bottom line, I couldn't afford to be stupid. I decided to follow her lead and try to keep my wits about me.

It was a moment before she spoke. Do you ever fantasize about going somewhere, starting over?

I think everybody has a some point.

Where would you go?

Anywhere?

How about anywhere we could go tonight? Grand Central's only a transfer away.

I think the trains have stopped running by now.

You kidding? It'd probably be morning rush by the time we got there.

We could take a train upstate and visit my family, since you're getting along so well.

That's not what I had in mind, she said softly.

... You want to hear something cool about Grand Central? You know the constellations on the ceiling? Well, the story goes, a little kid was studying astronomy in his science class and was passing through there with his family. He looked up, and a couple seconds later told his dad the whole thing was backwards. Sure enough, whoever painted the thing screwed up, but rather than fix it they just left it how it was.

Don't you have wishes?

Gulp. I reminded myself to keep it simple. Sure, I said.

What do you wish for?

What do you?

To see oceans. Islands. Don't you want to get out of this city, try something different?

What's wrong with New York?

What's good about it?

CONCRETE FEVER

She had me there. I hated the place. But I knew it inside and out. There was a neighborhood for whatever mood I was in. Didn't make it any less of a trash heap, but there were some areas I hated less than others. While I thought about how to phrase a response, I heard her laughing under her breath. Something funny? I asked.

Yuuup.

What?

You can't think of anything.

How about Riverside? You said...

Parks are an escape from the city. You can't list them as reasons why it's worth sticking around in.

Alright. The buildings.

The buildings?

Yeah. Where else are you going to find a skyline like ours?

How about any other city.

You ever gone to the top of the Empire State Building?

Have you?

No, but I was born here.

So why are you bringing it up?

Because somebody built that thing. Supposedly, it's inspiring.

You're the worst bullshitter I've ever met in my life. The only thing buildings ever brought New York was a bunch of tourists that don't know how to walk on a goddamn sidewalk. You get claustrophobic just living here. And you know this.

Yeah, but you hate buildings, you're shit out of luck. The whole country's being built up.

Not like here. Every day there's another billion dollar condo.

That's everywhere. You'd have to reach the Midwest before you'd find a place that's not happening.

Okay, so why don't we?

Why don't we what?

Move out of the city and go where there's room to breathe? We could catch a train and keep going.

I'd rather hitchhike actually. It'd be more sexy.

I'd be down for that!

We could sleep out under the stars until we could afford a trailer or something to live in. We'd get fake names so no one could find us. Get married in some small chapel, and settle down in a town so tiny it's not even on a map.

We could do whatever we wanted.

And whenever times got tight, we'd just sell off our children one by one to make ends meet. Barefoot and pregnant. That'd be the life, baby, you and me.

She went quiet, then asked, Why did you do that?

Do what?

Make a joke of it.

Were you being serious?

We could get a fresh start, find someplace that fits.

It would never work.

Why not?

I'm kind of dug in here.

You gotta be kidding.

What?

You were going to kill yourself! That's what this city did to you.

No, that's what life did to me, and it's not going to get any better, wherever I go.

Wherever we go.

Stop that.

CONCRETE FEVER

Stop what?
Pretending that...
I'm not pretending.
... I don't know what you want me to say.
Something honest.
I wish... I don't know! Why are you asking?
I want you to trust me... Talk to me!
I can't! I'm not scared with you. You... make me feel alright. And I haven't. For a long time. I talk about it I'm going to fuck it up.

A flashlight appeared fifty yards from where we were standing. It swept across the tunnel and came closer. We should go, I whispered.

No one's coming, she said.
Shhh! There's a MTA guy right over there.
No there's not. No one else exists.
Whatever. We're trespassing, we need to go back.
There's no one there. There's no one anywhere. It's just us.

The light paused, the worker still a ways off, searching an area just to our right. Then it flickered past and shot the opposite direction. I thought I'd catch at least a silhouette in the stoplights but didn't. I kept watching until it disappeared. The wind picked up from behind us, throwing a cloud of dust into the air. The stoplights turned yellow. Far off a set of brakes screeched.

She spiraled her nails over my arm, unfazed. If we could start over... leave everything behind?
Not now, okay?
Then when?
We need to move, there's a train coming.
This could be our chance.

I caught her expression in the yellow light and stopped. The eyeliner had smeared and black rivers ran down her cheeks.

We can get a fresh start, she repeated. You were honest with me.

I was, but...

That's all that matters.

Right now, we need to move.

I don't want to.

Do you want to die?

Do you?

I weighed her tone. It wasn't accusatory. It wasn't mocking. It was conspiratorial. Like if I said yes she'd stay planted there with me. The noise died in the station we'd left. A faint announcement could be heard. The stoplights went green. The brakes let up as the train rolled forward and the cry pierced my ears. I found her eyes. They hadn't left my face. Clarity hit. I shook my head. The slight gesture gave whatever permission she needed, and we moved to safety between the uprights. I wrapped her in my arms, gripping tighter as the train whipped past. Paranoia seized me, thinking her bag might catch. There wasn't room to check. I tried to pray. The noise made it impossible to think. My eyes throbbed, staring down the passing cars, tears spilling down my cheeks. Finally the last car shot out of sight, clamoring toward its next destination. The lights shot back to red.

Pressed there in silence, she plunged her hand south. She found me curled up into myself and asked if everything was okay. I told her I was fine. Just the night had worn me out was all.

CONCRETE FEVER

We discovered a staircase leading from the tracks to the platform and somehow arrived undetected. The fluorescent light was a shock. We stumbled blind for a moment. I led her to the exit. I craved breathable air. Instead I inhaled gravel. Ash. Brimstone.

It was still dark out. The night refused to end. I thought of asking Gypsy what time it was but suspected she trashed her phone hours ago. A few nondescript cars eased past, followed by a streetcleaner. A hotdog vendor set up shop. Overachiever business types entered glittering towers.

My stomach jolted. I knew the neighborhood, though I hadn't been there in years. I searched for a cab, there were none. I considered slugging down the rest of the flask to numb myself. Heading back underground to avoid the sight. Instead I found myself treading forward, Gypsy unsure but following. I knew I'd see it once I reached the corner. I continued nonetheless. My steps dragged to slow motion. Three to go. I tried to swallow but couldn't. Two to go. My throat bulged. Last step. The lump sank and my stomach flipped. Gypsy pulled alongside me. We silently stood and stared.

There was ground zero only a few blocks away, the digging crews in full swing. Police barricades and dumptrucks lining the avenue, warped girders sticking out their tops, awaiting transport to god knows where. Conscious effort had been made to block anyone from approaching the site. I could smell it though. Months later the air was still full of it. I slowly inhaled, pushing through the lingering burn. I stared into the worklights. Gypsy dug her nails into my palm but my mind was elsewhere. I'd already started planning how I was going to get past the cops and into the pit.

Nathaniel Kressen

Nathaniel Kressen

CONCRETE FEVER

Nix went schizophrenic those first weeks after the baby was born. One tireless voice pleaded with her to give up and get out. A second guilted her to no end. Called her heartless. Who fantasizes about abandoning a child less than a month after leaving the hospital? She was never meant to be a mother. She sucked at all things maternal. The baby cried when she held it, shut up when Jughead took over. Scowled when she spoke, smiled when he was there. Shit, pissed, and coughed up on her all day, then giggled the moment he came home. She'd carried this strange alien thing nine months inside her. Spent half a year in the same apartment, unable to paint, glued to a bed, gorged on daytime television. And after all that, now that it was out, it wanted nothing to do with her.

Jughead's upper crust parents were pure stereotype. They wore sweaters draped around their necks and white slacks in the summertime. They had perfect bronze tans from mornings spent sailing off the coast of Long Island. Gentle blonde hair. High cheekbones. Eyes so blue they set

159

Nix on edge. For a while they drove into the city every weekend to visit. Nix tried to be polite but they always stayed long past their welcome. One day she blurted out that the baby was getting claustrophobic from all the attention. They took the hint. The visits got less frequent, and only took place when Jughead was sure to be there.

They insisted Nix call them Bubby and Pop Pop. She couldn't tell if they were making fun of her own chosen name. When she asked Jughead he said they weren't. Just trying to welcome her into the family.

Jughead didn't touch a drop, meanwhile. Stopped heading out after work. His superiors didn't hold it against him, just chalked it up to the new baby at home. He never confided in Nix that he had discovered a balance through drinking he couldn't find otherwise. A certainty of purpose, of place. A blissful, smoked glass time-out from the world. The memory of it clawed at him. Nonetheless, he recognized the risks. He'd been splayed out in a bar booth when his child was born. He swore to make the change. It wasn't wrong thinking that one drink might lead to dozens, that it had the power to wreck his family beyond repair.

The baby's first Christmas came fast. Jughead got Nix an easel, canvases, and a host of painting supplies. She got him a silver flask specially imprinted with one of his art school sketches. Bubby and Pop Pop were in the tropics but sent a ton of gifts. Nix was surprised to see her name on one of the presents. The card read We Love You!, exclamation point and all. She tore through the wrapping and her jaw dropped. They'd given her a black pearl necklace. She studied them closer and shrieked. They were genuine, top quality, absolutely her style. More than she could ever afford. She dashed into the bathroom, clasped it around her neck and looked at herself in the mirror. She felt like royalty. It was the most anyone had ever spent on her.

Jughead leaned against the doorjamb. He'd wrapped a tie around his forehead and shoved a pair of cufflinks in his nostrils. He said something but it was indecipherable. He removed the cufflinks and asked, You like it?

It's incredible, she replied. I can't believe your parents...

They asked me to find out what kind of stuff you liked. So yeah. I'm a spy.

What did you tell them?

That you like things dark but classy, that you pretend you don't like expensive stuff but you do.

Lingering on her reflection, Nix counted the dark pearls against her pale complexion. I can't believe they did this. I feel bad. It must have cost them a fortune.

Come on, you know it's nothing to them.

Okay, but the money had to have come from somewhere.

Jughead frowned. So you don't like it?

No, I love it!

Then what's the problem?

Nothing, just... Shouldn't I feel guilty about this? I haven't exactly been the model daughter-in-law.

Okay, so change.

Change? Change what?

I don't know, whatever you think you're doing.

Is that why they bought me this, to force me to behave?

Jughead sighed. Can't it just be a nice gift?

It depends if there are strings attached.

What strings would there be?

I don't know, they're your parents!

Right. My parents. Not yours. You don't have to worry about my mom flipping on you the way yours did. They just want to be on good terms. I mean, we're all stuck together for life at this point. Might as well make the effort.

... You really know how to suck the fun out of a situation, you know that?

I was kidding, Nix! It was a gift! They love you.

No, she said, tugging absently at the necklace. They love the baby. Who couldn't? The kid's a fucking sunbeam. He more than makes up for whatever headaches I... Wait, where is he?

She dashed out of the bathroom but didn't see him. She searched every room of the apartment but he was nowhere. Jughead said something but her ears were pounding. The strength went out of her legs. Her boy was gone. Her child. Jughead guided her to a chair opposite the Christmas tree. One of the gift boxes rattled beside her. Jughead tilted it up to reveal the baby, perfectly fine, having the time of his life. She dove to the ground and took hold of him, covering his face with a flurry of kisses. He laughed. She'd never heard his laugh up close before. She fought the urge to cry. It was perfectly normal for a son to love his mother, she told herself. Jughead knelt to join them. They spent the next twenty minutes on the floor together, taking turns placing the box over their heads and falling in and out of hysterics. By the end Nix felt comfortable in the darkness. She knew that no matter how long she lingered, her family would be waiting to welcome her.

***

The boy turned one in no time. For Nix the year was a series of moments. A shrieking giggle the first time he pet a stranger's dog. An afternoon digging worms in Central Park. Clumsy attempts at walking. Playful baths in the sink. Drawing with wet fingertips on the mirror. It stunned her how long his limbs grew, how fast he absorbed information. The changes were imperceptible day-to-day, but doctor visits cemented the facts. The boy was thriving.

Soon he'll be running his father's firm, the doctor joked.

Not if I can help it, Gypsy playfully shot back.

Jughead got his promotion. The salary bump went toward a downpayment on a three-bedroom apartment. Nix was overjoyed having a studio space where she could work. She setup her easel and canvases before even thinking about clothing or kitchenware. She ignored his comments about it one day becoming a second child's bedroom. Another baby was the last thing on her mind.

It wasn't long until Nix despised the room. All of her time was spent caring for the boy and maintaining the house. He was a fitful sleeper, so nights and naptimes rarely provided opportunity to find a rhythm. On the rare occasions she got an hour to herself, she was too exhausted to create. The studio filled up with items that wouldn't fit anywhere else. Jughead suggested they get a dog, maybe a cat to start. He thought the baby would love it. She refused outright. The idea of finding paw prints dried into her paintings was enough to drive her insane.

Thanksgiving approached. Jughead's parents arrived the week before, and Nix suggested they stay in the apartment rather than find a hotel. Give them a chance to spend some time with the baby after their two month siesta in Mexico. When they arrived Nix blushed, unable to shake the suspicion that they'd recreated her first date with Jughead. Soon she was picturing her in-laws in all sorts of sexual positions. A mariachi band played a private concert while they engaged in a tequila fueled fit of passion. Oh Bubby! Oh Pop Pop! She snorted loudly. The conversation cut off and everyone turned to look at her. Jughead asked what had been so funny. She said that the baby had peed in her arms and excused the both of them hurriedly. She held her shirt under the faucet to validate her story, then threw it in the laundry. She changed his diaper unnecessarily. She composed herself and rejoined the rest.

Bubby and Pop Pop slept in the studio. It didn't take much effort to clear space, sadly. It only took relocating some blank canvases and the last unpacked boxes from the move. While Nix dressed the pullout couch Bubby politely remarked on an old piece hanging on the wall. You have a real eye, dear. You should have really stuck with it.

I did. I mean, I am. Just, with the baby...

Of course, I didn't mean to presume. Is that, um, is that what I think it is?

Oh, that? Could be. I kind of lost track to be honest. Past life and all.

Bubby hesitated, smiled, then left to rejoin the men. Nix cursed herself for yet again saying the wrong thing. She made a mental note to wear the necklace for Thanksgiving dinner.

The day before the holiday, Nix planned to pick up the turkey she'd reserved. She was leaving the apartment when Jughead called from his office to say his boss would be coming to dinner as well. He was in the midst of a divorce and had nowhere else to go, he explained. Since he was an old colleague of Pop Pop's, the offer was only natural.

Nix gritted her teeth. One problem.

What's that?

We only have food for four.

You're going to the store. Pick something up.

Everything's sold out, it's the day before Thanksgiving!

Cook whatever. No one's expecting a revelation, Jughead teased. At some point they'd reclaimed the phrase as their own private joke.

Nix relented. Fine. It's just him, right?

Well, actually his girlfriend is coming, too. But it's fine, she weighs like ninety pounds. She'll probably have a carrot stick and pass out.

Anyone else? Nix asked pointedly.

With a southern drawl he replied, I think that's all, sweetie pie.

Don't try and charm me.

Aw shucks, sugah. You know what that tone does to me.

Uh-huh.

You're my darlin'. Just my sparklin' little star in the sky.

I'm hanging up now.

Vaya con dios, cowgirl.

She hung up the phone and couldn't help smiling. Thank god he's cute, she thought. She called goodbye to the baby, Bubby, and Pop Pop in the other room and left.

The neighborhood was empty on the way to the supermarket. City turned ghost town. She guessed most people had fled back to the suburbs from which they'd come. A gust of wind hit her and she pulled shut her coat. Her thoughts turned to her mother, as they often did. She tried writing a few times but the letters came back unopened. Jughead suggested they fly down to visit, have her meet her grandson. Nix said she would consider it but had no real intention of doing so. The idea fell off his radar. Nix had plenty of reasons why going down was the wrong move, but only one truly mattered. She knew that if she were in her mother's position, with her set of values, she'd behave in exactly the same way.

As expected, the shelves in the grocery store were picked clean. A crowd of people nonetheless crammed the aisles in search of last minute solutions. She fought her way to the butcher counter to pick up her turkey, then thought better of it. Now that she had to hunt the aisles for extra supplies, it would be better to grab it afterwards. Otherwise some rabid single mother might knock her senseless and gallop out of the store to parts unknown, hoisting the bird overhead in triumph.

Nix? a voice said behind her.

She turned and recognized a former classmate from art school. She instantly remembered her sprawling oil paintings. For a time they'd had a friendly competition over who could fill the larger canvas. She chose mundane subjects but her technique had always been solid. Nix was happy to notice she looked just the same. Tattoos crawling down her arms, three rings in each eyebrow. Oversized ripped clothing and black studded boots. It was like seeing a former version of herself.

It's Beth. From studio...? That is you, right?

Yeah, Nix answered. Hi, how are you?

Good! Trying the whole domestic thing for Thanksgiving this year. Probably makes me a huge loser, right?

CONCRETE FEVER

Uh, no. Not at all.

All I could find was a jar of olives, Beth said. I think the best move is going to be finding a liquor store and buying a handle of vodka. That way we can have dirty martinis all holiday long. Definitely something to be thankful for.

Nix's mouth slid into a grin. She'd just found her salvation from the capitalists. Hey, um, if you're interested, we're having a couple people over at our place. We have plenty of food.

You're still with Picasso, right?

Excuse me?

We all called him Picasso. Majorly talented. Plus his real name is so awful.

Well it's my name too now, so...

Beth's eyes widened. You didn't marry him, did you?!

Was I not supposed to do that?

I guess it's fine. I mean, as long as you're happy.

We have a little boy...

They spent a few minutes mooning over wallet photos and lamenting how old they were getting as other shoppers pushed past. In the end Beth said she would definitely come for the dinner, along with her boyfriend Nelson, another one of the artists from their program. Soon as they parted Nix realized it must be their final year of school. The graduating class held a high profile gallery show each year. She wondered what Beth and Nelson were planning. They must be in full swing heading into winter break, she thought. She forced herself to stop daydreaming. Housewives were hitting her on all sides. Women, she corrected herself. They're just like me, probably have a thousand things going on besides cooking for their in-laws and cleaning up barf all day. She picked up the turkey, stunned it was the same one she'd reserved. It looked less than half the size she remembered. Without a word of protest she headed to the cashier, wondering what in the hell she was going to feed a group now doubled in size.

The next morning was spent cooking. Nix and Bubby fell into an easy rhythm by their third hour sharing a kitchen. Thanks to Bubby's years of experience, everything was staggered to finish around the same time. Jughead and Pop Pop ignored their cleaning assignments to play legos with the boy and watch college football. Minutes before the guests were scheduled to arrive, Nix pulled the plug and insisted they get to work. She left Bubby in charge and took the baby to get dressed. She laid the baby down on the bed and slipped into a dress she'd saved for a special occasion. Five months on the hanger, under plastic, untouched. It fit perfectly. She put on the black pearls. She stood and examined herself. For once she couldn't think of a single criticism. It looked like the holiday would turn out alright after all.

A noise caught her attention. The baby's stomach growling. She looked and noticed a weird tension in his eyes. She heard his stomach again and realized Jughead must have forgotten to change him. She opened the diaper but found nothing. False alarm, she said as she pinched his cheek. Poor little guy has a tummy ache. Just then another rumble came from his stomach, and before she knew it a projectile shitstorm of biblical proportions shot out from the tiniest of sources and stuck to everything in its path.

Shocked into catatonia, it took the first door buzzer to revive her. She screamed for her husband, but Jughead called that his boss was on the way up. She kept screaming, and finally Bubby appeared.

Oh no! she said. Don't worry dear, we'll send that necklace to be cleaned for you.

Nix stared back, coated head to toe.

I'll take care of the little one. You just shower up and don't worry about a thing. The food is ready. Everyone's drinking and having fun. You're a wonderful host!

Nix retreated to the bathroom, eyes avoiding the mirror. She pulled off her dress and dropped it in the sink. She watched Bubby clean and change the baby. The door buzzed again. Conversation rose from the living room. Bubby hummed a soft tune, hoisted the baby onto her hip, and headed back to the party.

The shower drowned out any sound from the living room. She took her time, more than a little shaken. Out there were her husband's boss, her husband's parents, and their old classmates, still chasing their dreams. She'd done everything to prove she could handle the pressure. Play the perfect host. Show everyone what a good life they'd built for themselves. She peeled back the curtain and watched the mirror fog up. She reached over, wrote her real name, then smudged it out. She pulled the curtain shut and leaned against the wall. Focused on the drops sliding over her scar, over freckles and blemishes. She realized how pale her skin was. Not unusual for November but it bothered her all the same. Her body was a blank canvas. Gathering dust. She fought the urge to drag a knife over it.

She dried off, anxious to return. She picked an outfit and dressed quickly. At the end of the hallway she paused to glance around the corner. Jughead's boss was tossing and catching the baby, who was laughing uncontrollably. He was tall and manicured, wearing a tailored suit and sporting slicked back hair. His girlfriend was Nix's age, maybe younger. She was rail skinny with a puckered mouth and bleached blonde hair. Nix groaned, suddenly dreading the next few hours. Bubby and Pop Pop were beside the two of them, smiling. Beth sat at the far end of the room with Nelson, who looked like he'd dropped an unhealthy amount of weight since the last time she'd seen him. They drank dirty martinis out of rocks glasses and grimaced at the fits and squeals dominating the room. Nix remembered how she used to think about kids and instantly felt grateful they'd come. She looked around but couldn't locate Jughead. When she finally entered into the living room nobody noticed. Everyone was watching the baby. She slid past her in-laws and into the kitchen.

Bubby had dumped a bottle of blue cheese dressing into the salad. Nix had expressly told her not to. There would be dressing on the table, people could add their own. She'd spent an hour boiling and cutting the root vegetables, slicing the tomatoes, peppers, and cauliflower, tossing the greens. Now all of them were swallowed in a nauseating white puddle that reached halfway up the bowl. She went to trash the whole mess but stopped shy of the bin. With great effort she returned the salad to the counter and focused on happy thoughts.

Jughead burst in the door, carrying four bags of ice. Hi, sweetie! shouted Bubby. He grunted and pushed past his mother into the kitchen.

Where were you? Nix asked.

Nelson brought two handles of vodka.

We have ice.

Not enough.

Those aren't going to fit in the freezer.

Jughead sighed. What about the fridge?

CONCRETE FEVER

The fridge?!
Why not?
It'll melt!
I don't know, I was trying to help. I didn't even invite them.
Would you keep your voice down?
You're the one freaking out, he said in hushed voice.
I am not. And they're your friends too.
I never said they weren't.
You're the one that turned our apartment into a country club. And now your mother's sabotaging my dinner...
My parents like you, you know.
I like them too.
Jughead narrowed his eyes.
Nix gritted her teeth. I asked them to stay with us, didn't I?
... You want to hit me right now, don't you?
No. Maybe a little. It's just the day. I wish your boss would stop throwing our child in the air.
He kissed her forehead. Everything okay now?
Sure. Great, she said, monotone. He opened the freezer. There's no room in there.
Just checking.
I told you though. There was no reason to check.
Alright, my mistake.
I'm getting really tired of people in your family not listening to me.
Jughead suddenly pulled a knife out of the cutting block, slit open the bags, and dumped them into the sink. The ice spilled out onto the countertop. The noise drew everyone's attention. Get it before it melts! he said. He

glared back at Nix, then shot an ice cube basketball style into the trash.

Look, we're both stressed, Nix said, slowly taking the knife out of his hand. Why don't you have a drink and relax?

His eyes darted to the vodka, sinking back into his head.

Come on, I'll make it for you.

Jughead didn't answer, just kept shooting cubes. None of them went in.

Nix sighed, grabbed herself a glass and ice from the sink, then headed to make herself a cocktail. Within seconds Beth was at her side. Some crowd, she said.

You should have been here earlier. I got shit on.

Like, actual shit?

We know how to party.

Everyone! Bubby called out. Now that we're all assembled let's take our seats, shall we?

Nix shot a look at her mother-in-law, who didn't seem to notice, then headed to the table with everyone else. The place settings had been rearranged. The blue cheese salad sat in central focus. Would anyone care to say grace? Bubby asked.

Nix snorted loudly, thinking it was a joke. The table stared at her. She pretended to have something stuck in her throat and slouched lower in her seat, coughing. Bubby pressed on, asking Jughead to do the honors. He caught eyes with Nix, then turned back to his mother and nodded. Everyone clasped their hands on the table, even Beth and Nelson who likely felt they had no other choice. Nix however kept hers buried in her lap, confident her husband was going to subvert the whole thing somehow.

CONCRETE FEVER

Jughead cleared his throat. Thank you Lord for this bountiful meal. For good family and friends. For our baby boy who reminds us every day how precious life is. And for my wife Nix, who I know has your blessing. Give us the strength to weather hard times and treasure the good. Amen.

The Amen echoed around the table. Lively conversation sprang up and plates got passed around. Nix would only recall moments from the meal. The voices in her head clamored nonstop. You should jump out the window, they teased. That'd break up this little yuppie paradise. Jughead's boss asked her questions. She botched every answer. Beth shot her looks but was stuck at the other end of the table. Nelson looked ready to off himself. Jughead looked perfectly at home.

That night Jughead rolled over and said he was in the mood. She reminded him of his parents in the next room. He said he didn't care. She said, What was that toast about?

At dinner?

You used the word bountiful.

I'm sorry you didn't enjoy it.

You don't have to act clean-cut just because they're staying with us.

My boss was here.

So you can't be yourself?

And who would that be? he asked.

I don't know, she said. Maybe the man I married.

He got up, pulled a pack of cigarettes from the dresser and opened the window. He took a long drag and stared out at the night. Another drag.

I thought you quit, she said.

I can't quit everything at once.

Nathaniel Kressen

What's that supposed to mean?

Do you have any idea how hard it was for me sitting there? Watching everyone sip their drinks, care-free?

You're not an alcoholic.

How do you know?

Because you're more interesting when you drink. You're not this religious freak robot, I'll tell you that much.

I don't know what to tell you. I can't grow my hair long and sleep till noon every day just so you can pretend we're still in college. It's a good job... I'm good at it, Nix.

You're good at everything. It's a disease. You'd probably make a good alcoholic if you wanted to. But you're not some corporate type!

He exhaled sharply. That meal you worked so hard to make, that everyone complimented you on... You think we could have done any of that without my job?

Doesn't matter. You mother sabotaged it.

Jughead stubbed out the rest of his cigarette and closed the window. Alright, I'm done.

Excuse me?

He pulled on his clothes from earlier.

Where are you going?

Out.

No you're not.

Are you going to stop me? His question shook the air. It wasn't particularly loud, but there was a venom in it that crystallized and put them both on edge. He clasped his pants shut and tied his shoes. Grabbed a sweater and coat from hooks on the wall. At the bedroom door he paused. Nix watched him silently from the bed, exposed. The blanket fallen off her. If I don't leave I'm going to drink the rest of that handle, he said. Then he eased open the door and disappeared. She listened to his labored steps tread through the kitchen and out of the apartment.

***

First word. Full sentences. Bigger clothes. Toilet training. Playgroup. Allergies. Trips to the ER. Races through the apartment. Hard-fought detox from the baby bottle. The thrill of motherhood came in spurts over the next year. The exhaustion never quit. Nix rarely saw Jughead. He was sober but worked long hours at the office. When they did see each other all she talked about was wanting to paint. Finally he went ahead and hired a nanny to look after the boy. Nix would sit in the studio staring at blank canvases, hours on end. Inevitably, when inspiration hit, she'd hear her baby cry and rush to see what was the matter. Even in silence she felt profound guilt for handing him over to a complete stranger. Within a week she fired her. She decided she must have romanticized the memories of her past life. If she'd been destined to create something of substance, she would have done it.

She and Jughead stopped talking. When he got home he collapsed on the opposite end of the couch, asked a few questions about the boy and fell asleep in front of the TV. Every two weeks he got the urge to sleep with her. He made attempts at romance but she saw through them. She knew he only wanted her so he could shoot one off and rest easy another couple weeks. She got paranoid he was trying to get her pregnant again. She started refusing him altogether. In time they stopped kissing. They were more like roommates waiting out the end of a lease.

One day Nix opened an invitation to Beth's gallery opening. The grad show had been a success and she'd received interest from dealers. The event was in a Chelsea venue with a big reputation. Early twenties and she was already a featured artist. Nix determinedly smiled for her friend's success until her cheeks hurt. She splashed water on her face and kept scrubbing grass stains out of the boy's play pants.

They got a sitter. It'd been a while since they'd gone out. She wore her best dress and applied make-up. He wore his clothes from work that day. He opened the window on the cab ride down to smoke a cigarette. She asked him to close it so her hair wouldn't get messed up. When did you start caring about that? he asked.

She didn't answer. In her hand she held a newspaper clipping.

What's that?

The write-up for her show, she said.

Good?

Sounds contrived. She stuffed the article into her purse and looked away.

He lit a cigarette and exhaled out the open window.

They found Nelson outside without a coat on. He was shivering and looking even more sickly thin than when he was at their apartment . Nix tried to get a few words out of him but couldn't. Jughead motioned for her to go inside. As she did she turned to watch Jughead offer up his suit jacket and sit down beside him.

The gallery was filled to capacity. She got stuck in a pack of tall people and couldn't figure out where to go. She got a glimpse of the artwork through their arms but couldn't get any closer. She pushed in random directions until she finally found Beth, surrounded by journalists. She'd ditched the drab clothing. In its place she wore a transparent silk evening gown. Her nipples showed through as did her more intimately placed tattoos. Nix got lost looking at one of a matador whose red cape distinctly beckoned the viewer to charge south.

Beth saw her and shouted, You made it!

Yeah, this is amazing.

Isn't it crazy? I think everyone turned out to see my nipples, personally.

It's quite a dress.

Have you looked at the pieces yet?

No, it's so packed, I...

Let me know what you think, okay? She gave her a tight hug, then returned to the journalists. Nix stood there unsure if she'd been dismissed. After a few seconds she fought toward the closest wall, figuring she'd start her lap from there. A few feet away she smelled something she couldn't place. Turned out to be the rotting carcass of a Thanksgiving turkey, suspended from the ceiling by a noose. Behind it was a large black and white portrait of a man and woman holding a baby. It was singed around the edges, as though someone had lit it on fire then changed their mind. Painted underneath were the contorted howling figures of condemned souls. The title of the piece was "The American Dream Killed My Artistic Self: No. 9."

It wasn't until the third piece that she saw a pattern. She made the full lap to be sure, getting more and more furious. She went outside to tell Jughead but he was gone. The gallery was flooding with people, there was a line to get back in. He could be anywhere in there, she thought. She decided to confront Beth herself.

It took twenty minutes to reach her. In the interim, she'd removed her panties from underneath the dress, revealing not only the last of her goods but also the word Ole! tattooed across her pelvis. The dueling conversations hit Nix from all directions and made her feel seasick. She had to wave to get Beth's attention.

You're a bitch! Nix shouted.

What? Beth shouted back.

You're. A. Bitch!

It's so loud in here!

What were you thinking?!

I'm glad you liked them, Beth said. Let's catch up another time, okay? The Times is here!

The crowd imploded and Nix got pushed backward. She considered stealing the turkey. In the end she waited outside for Jughead to come out. She cursed herself for not bringing an extra set of keys. After an hour in the cold she saw him walking up the sidewalk with a drunk Nelson on his arm. Where have you been? she demanded.

Nelson needed to talk.

He didn't want to talk when I saw him.

Did you ever talk in class?

I've been waiting for over an hour.

Jughead reached the front of the gallery and lowered Nelson to sit against the entrance. He straightened up and rotated to crack his spine.

She eyed him. You smell like alcohol.

We went to a bar.

What happened to staying sober?

Here's the thing...

CONCRETE FEVER

I don't want to hear it, she interrupted. Did he tell you what Beth did? She took our life and make an exhibit out of it.

I thought it was an abstract.

There's a turkey carcass hanging in front of a photo of the all-American family.

And you think that's us.

Do you clean up kid shit all day? Cause I do. Tons of it. Day in, day out. Shit, shit, shit. If that's not the American Dream you tell me what is.

I'm going to find Beth that Nelson is outside.

You're not going to reach her. She's too busy flashing her vagina. Giving handjobs to journalists.

Jughead eyed her, then went inside.

Before long they were in a cab riding back to the apartment. So I guess you're drinking again, Nix said bitingly.

Do you actually want to talk about it?

I don't know what there is to say.

... Nelson was really upset. Beth's a different person. He needed someone to talk to. So I had a drink. I sat there watching him down drink after drink, but I only had the one.

Am I supposed to congratulate you?

This is huge, Nix. I thought I would lose control...

You could have. You risked whatever you thought was at stake just because Beth's being a cold heartless bitch.

That's not the reason he's upset.

Like I give a shit, Nix said. The ride ended in silence.

After the sitter left, Nix launched back into her indictment of the exhibit. Jughead milled about the apartment. Are you even listening?! she asked, fuming.

Do you want me to respond?

Yes.

I always thought Beth was a good artist. I'm not surprised she's successful.

Nix's eyes widened. Her back stiffened. She turned away without responding.

Come on, sweetie.

Don't call me sweetie.

Excuse me?

How do you see me? A wife? A mother? An artist?

You're all of those.

Not the last one so much though.

I tried helping with that.

No, you knocked me up.

Jughead fought to keep his composure. Don't talk like that about our son.

We're not having another one. You know that, right? I'm not going through this again.

I don't know how to talk to you when you're like this.

No, you don't know how to listen, she said. I'm telling you, no more kids.

Look, I know you've been under a lot of pressure.

What pressure am I under? I sit home all day.

Nix...

You're the one with the job. You're the one supporting us.

You're a good mother. Our son adores you. And one day, when we're ready...

You ever want to have sex again, you get snipped, got me?

Jughead stopped a second, stuck on how his wife said the word sex with a disgusted look on her face. Then he said, There are other options. Ones less permanent. You don't know how you're going to feel in another couple of years. There's always the pill.

Never again. Chemicals make me crazy.

Can't imagine what that'd be like, he said before thinking better of it. Her face contorted, she choked back a sob, and slammed the bedroom door in his face. The boy woke up and called from his room. Jughead went in there to comfort him. He feel asleep brushing the hair from his forehead.

Months earlier, a college grad named Mindy got hired by Jughead's office. She was a hell of a stock broker, one of the few women in the field. Smart as a whip, understated beauty, a soft temper with eyes to get lost in. But Jughead was spoken for. They had casual conversations in the office, took walks to grab coffee, talked abstractly about getting together some night after work. She knew he was married, he mentioned Nix in almost every conversation. He had no interest in anything happening. He loved his wife. He just appreciated the human contact, having lived like a monk for longer than he cared to admit.

The Monday following the gallery opening, Mindy noticed Jughead unusually quiet. She asked if he wanted to go out for a drink after work and talk about it. He considered, then agreed. She proved to be a drinker. Raised in Texas, she could hold her liquor with the best of them. They reached a solid buzz around the same time, about an hour and a half in. By then they were laughing. Jughead was on the verge of finding his place. They got closer and closer until their heads touched. She smelled like jasmine. They stayed there, talking at random, other times staying silent with their temperatures pulsing upward, neither of them having the strength to pull away.

He got home late. Nix had spent the better part of an hour putting the boy to bed. She never figured out how to tell bedtime stories. He was waiting for you, she said as he entered the apartment.

He set his keys down and hung up his coat. She was going on and on about something, it all sounded like one long vowel to him. He stretched his arms toward her but she backed away saying he stunk of alcohol. She was about to launch into another damnation of him when he quietly said, I did something.

She was thrown by his tone and stopped mid-sentence.

I, I went for a drink. With someone. From work.

He expected her to stop him. She didn't. He fought through the lingering drunk to keep going.

It was just cause, I haven't been able to talk to you. For so long.

What are you talking about?

I love you, Nix.

What did you do?

Nix...

Did you fuck somebody?

Jughead jolted out of his prepared confession and stared.

Nix clasped her hands behind her head and walked away. Oh god, she said.

Wait, he cried.

Nix was pacing.

I didn't do it, he said.

Then what did you do?

We touched heads.

Excuse me?

We just leaned our heads together. For a while.

CONCRETE FEVER

You didn't fuck her?

No.

And you didn't kiss her?

He shook his head.

Why are you telling me this?

Because I love you. And the whole time, I wanted it to be you.

You're drunk.

I want you to come back to me Nix.

Did you want to fuck her? I bet you did. You know what? Call her up. Go fuck her. Because this drunk spineless clean-cut sonofabitch you've become is not someone I want in the lives of me or my son.

... What, what are you saying?

I think that was pretty clear.

I just said I loved...

Get the fuck out.

Without knowing how it happened Jughead was at another bar. He downed drink after drink. Thinking. He was sure his head would be the end of him. He found his perfect drunk and kept going until it burned down and he was in the throws of a violent sick. He couldn't read the bill at closing time. He was sure it was astronomical. Suddenly he remembered he had work in a few hours. He stumbled out the front entrance and managed to find his way back to the apartment. He stumbled to the bedroom closet. He pulled at an armful of suits still on their hangers. He tugged full force until the bar broke from the wall and everything came crashing down. The noise woke Nix who immediately started pushing Jughead out the bedroom, down the hallway, and toward the front door. At the living room he realized the work clothes he'd come for had fallen and scattered. He bent to pick them up but Nix kept pushing. She screamed every inflammatory word she could think of. He couldn't take it. In the fog of his drunk he turned wildly and smacked her to the ground. Momentarily sober, he saw the love of his life lying there and realized he was to blame. It'd always been coming. Only a matter of time before he lost control. He dropped the last of his clothes, fumbled to get the apartment key off his chain, and placed it on the surface he could find. He wanted her to be healthy. To be free of him if that was what she wanted. He wanted her to be happy. In the capsized room he caught sight of a small figure in blue. He staggered toward it. He desperately wanted to comb the hair from its forehead. His breath labored out and he knew he was about to be sick. He had to get out. Without a word he found his way to the door and exited the apartment.

Nix tested her cheek and found it hot. She nonetheless poked at it. She felt her son's eyes. She was infinitely thankful he was too young to remember this. She promised he'd never witness anything like it again. He'd lead a perfect life. The both of them would. She peeled herself off the floor and tried to smile for her son. It hurt but she managed. She stared absently at the pajamas she'd folded a dozen times or more. For the first time she noticed how wrong the airplanes' flight patterns were. They looked ready to crash any second.

CONCRETE FEVER

Thousands of New Yorkers died. Millions more were affected. The city decided to pay tribute by building the spacebeams from Independence Day. While I didn't exactly catch every vigil on television, I was nonetheless pissed they were going to construct a pair of blue hard-ons as a backdrop. Ratings would soar. Stoners nationwide would tune in. All to see Will Smith running down the Canyon of Heroes to save the day. When I heard the plans, I couldn't stop picturing my father's corpse rising from the destruction. Floating into the clouds. Destined for a long bout of alien probing. After a while I indulged the fantasy. It helped push down the sickness and I never had to feel anything except a general sense of disappointment.

The Tribute in Light was still a few months from completion. At least that's what the families were told. Some took it hard, convinced there were still survivors under the wreckage. It was impossible at that point, but I didn't judge. Everyone dealt with it in their own way. I did my best not to think about it. Dead was dead.

Nathaniel Kressen

Standing so close to the site though, it was hard not to feel affected. The image of his corpse became one of his soul. I envisioned blue highways guiding him upward. Into a place he couldn't get bombed back out of.

Without a word we walked north on Broadway along the barricades. The sidestreets on our left slid downhill toward the site. All of them closed off. Between were stretches of fast food and discount retail. Grates drawn over the storefronts. Memories of dust in the hinges. We reached St. Paul's Cathedral, looking massive against its apocalyptic surroundings. Gypsy stopped at the wrought iron fence. Every inch of it was covered in banners and flags. Letters, photos, drawings. I Heart NY shirts. FDNY hats. Before I knew it I was reading even the tiniest writing by the glow of the streetlight.

Then we were inside. Relief and rescue workers filled the pews. Exhausted. Drawn thin. Praying. A priest consoled someone with vacant eyes. They held a silent horror. I doubted words could break it. We passed a group of volunteers rapidly speaking in hushed tones. A few seconds painted a stark picture. The cots upstairs were filled to capacity. Chiropractors worked twelve-hour shifts, but were still turning away half the people seeking treatment. Donations arrived from around the world, but there was no more space to store them. Respirator masks. Hardhats. Gloves, boots, socks. Band-aids. Aspirin. Gum. One woman said they received 290,000 tubes of chapstick. They were going back out at a rate of 700 a day.

We trudged out the back of the cathedral, which opened out into a the graveyard. One of the oldest in the city. A freezing cold wind hit us full force. We continued nonetheless, dodging scattered patches of ice on the walkway. A rescue worker approached us heading the opposite direction. The blackened equipment hung heavy on him. He pulled off a pair of soaked gloves. Steam lingered in a cloud around his hands. He drew a soiled rag from his pocket and wiped the sweat off his face.

Gypsy opened her mouth to say something but I stopped her. I wanted to pass undetected. She shot me a look, then paused to watch him vanish into the cathedral. When she turned and saw the viewing platform, she stopped in her tracks. I didn't hear they...

Last month, I said.

We started walking through the gravesites. Centuries old. Leaning odd angles. The inscriptions worn off. You ever notice, Gypsy said, That people never show emotion when they bury someone? It's always beloved this and beloved that. You'd think they'd be more original.

I can't read any of these.

I can't either. I just mean in general.

The wind picked up, howling. I heard my name again. No more than a whisper. I decided to ignore it. I'd already risked her life once trying to track it down.

You hear that wind? she asked. It sounds like voices.

... Are you messing with me?

All the souls were out flying because of the full moon. Now they have to get back before sunrise.

Can we not talk like that?

Hey, it's your funeral. Get it? Cause we're in a graveyard...?

I glanced back. Everyone was either in the cathedral or in the pit. We were alone there, surrounded by corpses. I could see the outlines of clouds above us. I figured the sun must be somewhere close. I'm going, I said.

Nathaniel Kressen

Where?
I motioned to the site ahead.
Are you nuts?
I have to.
You're never going to get better if you keep torturing yourself.
Who says I want to get better?
I do.
I was ready to jump tonight.
You didn't.
You stopped me.
Didn't take much, she scoffed.
I righted myself. You were ready to stand in the tracks.
Yeah, because I was choosing something.
How does that make any sense?
You wanted to jump because you were giving up. You lost faith. I found it.
I reached for my flask. She snatched it out my hand and stuffed it into her bag.
You think it's coincidence we ended up here? she asked. Not pausing for a response, she asked, We're meant to have a second chance.
I'm not going to kill myself, alright?
I didn't think you were.
Than what's the problem?
There are cops up there. I get seen, I go back.
You're going to have to go home at some point anyway.
She took a step back. Her eyes shifted. Finally she said, You were never going to leave with me, were you?
What, like leave, leave?
The city. All this. Start a life together.

... Look, I know whatever's going on is probably bad, alright? I get it.

She bore her knuckles into her temples. The muscles in her neck constricted. She bit her lip white.

Your dad has to ease up eventually, I said.

How dare you joke about that shit?! she exploded. I don't joke about your dead father.

What are you talking about? Your dad's not...

Shut up! They beat me there, you know that? The caretakers, the other orphans. I can't even sleep without...

Gypsy...?

Get away from me! I don't even know who the fuck you are!

I took her in my arms. She bucked against me, then reached into my jacket and stole the letters. She twisted my nipple and slid out of my grasp. She considered the letters a moment, then ripped them down the middle.

What are you doing?!

You're tied to this fantasy, she said. You need to be set free.

Those were my father's!

She tore them smaller and smaller, circling behind a grave to avoid me. Then she threw them into the air. The pieces flew every direction as I watched helpless. One clump caught briefly against the face of a gravestone, then whipped out of sight with the rest.

We have this window, she said in an even tone. We can escape. It's going to be close. We don't have long. Grand Central's going to open and we're going to get away.

What are you...?

She smiled, suddenly oblivious. I had a rocking horse. Found it in the trash, if you can believe it. It won't fit in a suitcase. We'll have to carry it.

Listen to me...

I saw this documentary once about a pair of scuba divers. They dove so deep, they said the pressure could split open their lungs. But they kept right on going. Kept on diving till they found...

We're not going anywhere!

She looked away.

Why did you do that? I yelled, breathless. You knew what those meant!

They meant nothing, she said.

... What is this? Are you playing with me or are you actually...?

I'm playing.

You sure?

It's all a game.

I looked at the site. I couldn't imagine how many unnamed bodies were still buried there. Then I noticed the cop by the platform entrance staring at us, about forty yards away. My stomach sank, thinking how our conversation must have carried.

Do you hear those voices? she asked, tears in her eyes. Like whispers. You can almost feel the souls flying around. I bet they're cutting through us right now and we can't even tell.

Stop it, alright?

It's over, Jumper. I'm done.

I felt a bullet enter my back. It dug through to my chest and exploded my organs one by one. I started to sink. I looked behind me but there was no one there.

What do we have? she asked. No fireworks, no magic...

That's not true, I said, struggling for air.

Why don't you tell me what's so special then?

I reached for her hand and she jerked away. Her eyes were so alert they scared me. Somehow I expected them to empty.

I can't play the part of the perfect girlfriend, she said. I've been touched so many times by so many sets of hands, I can't remember them all. You're just one out of a million. I've been passed around this whole city.

My words welled up in my throat. I stood there watching her cry.

This was never meant to be something, she said. If we don't cut it off now, before we get invested, it's going to explode right in our faces.

I don't think that, I said, finally managing the words.

I'm not getting hurt like that.

We're in this together.

No we're not.

She started to leave. I grabbed her. Maybe a little too rough given the circumstance. She convulsed, I tightened my grip, both of us yelled nonsense. What is it, I'm not strong enough? Is that it?!

It was your game, Jumper, it didn't mean anything...

I'll be whatever you want me to, alright?

You fooled yourself with love...

You want me to dominate you I'll dominate you...

You fooled yourself with love...

I'll become everything I'm scared of for you!

You fooled yourself with...

I took hold of her wrists and tried to pin her down between the gravestones. She proved too wild to control and fought me from her knees. I knew the cop would get there any second but I couldn't think straight.

Get off me! she yelled.

You want this, I know you do.

Get off me! Stop it!

Suddenly there was a switchblade an inch in front of my face. I released her. She scrambled to her feet, I rose slowly. I checked for the cop but he'd left his post. I heard a distant set of shoes running on salted concrete. Gypsy's eyes flickered but settled back on me.

She rotated the knife slightly and said, We're calling this quits before it gets awkward.

I fought the lump in my throat and pleaded, Don't do this.

You feel the souls creeping back in? One by one, coming back home?

Don't do this.

Little by little, more and more, filtering in.

I love you.

Her face registered nothing. I must have swallowed the words, I thought. Hard as it was, I decided to confess again. Before I could she said, You felt something for me, that's your fault.

Beyond her I could see the cop entering the graveyard. Behind me I heard raised voices from the cathedral. I could only think of one way out. I limped toward her, my ankle once again throbbing. I locked eyes, begging her to plunge the blade into me. She didn't. I grabbed for the knife to do it myself but missed. Her lips opened slightly. Her eyes lost their edge. No hint of what just happened. I waited for her to say something but she stayed silent.

CONCRETE FEVER

You're the one that's sick, I told her. Look for me on the concrete.

***

The police took her inside, out of sight. They questioned me against a cop car. Kept the engine running. For effect, I guess. I knew the only thing that scared Gypsy was getting sent home. I honestly couldn't care less what they did with me. I'd lost all momentum. I sat on the ground but they made me stand back up. I watched the black fumes spill from the tailpipe and dance briefly before evaporating into nothing. Seemed as fitting a metaphor as anything for the way the night went.

The officer who handcuffed me was a veteran on the force. Showed in his wrinkles, his budding gut, his depleted posture. Damned if I ever end up like that, I thought. Better to go out on top, while I still had sex appeal. You want to tell me what happened? he asked.

The wife and I are visiting from Albania, I said without attempting an accent. Came to see the twin towers.

You think this is funny?

Not at all, officer. The guidebook said they'd be here. I'm demanding my money back.

No response.

... So how about this night, huh? Like, where the hell's the sunrise, am I right?

The officer eyed me, then left.

I called out, So if you're done with me, can you unlock these? Two cops materialized on either side of me. How you boys doing? I asked. They didn't bother looking at me. I leaned against the car and stared at the sky. When the officer returned I'd thought up a few more smart-ass comments for him.

Your father died in the attacks? he asked, shocking me into silence. He motioned toward the cathedral. Your girlfriend.

I nodded dumbly. Tower Two.

He worked there?

I nodded.

What was happening when the officer arrived?

We were having an argument. It's... complicated.

She told us you defended her against an abusive ex-boyfriend earlier tonight. Is that where you got the bruises...? Believe me, playing tough is going to get you nowhere.

I didn't respond.

Why don't you describe him for me?

Dark hair. White. Late 20's probably. Built like a fucking gorilla.

Where did he approach her?

73rd, between Amsterdam and Columbus.

How did you get involved?

I hesitated, then answered, We were on a date.

He raised an eyebrow. At your apartment?

I work fast.

He turned to cough, then looked toward the site a minute. I waited for whatever was going to happen next. She's a nice girl, he said finally. Speaks a whole lot better of you than expected, given the situation.

What's she saying? I asked.

What's your name? he countered.

Didn't they show you my ID?

They did.

So you know already.

Why don't you tell me?

I don't like my name.

Listen, you can talk to me or you can talk to someone at the station. Your call.

Isn't that why you put these cuffs on me?

They're just a precaution.

Well, I'm not dangerous.

You been living with your mother since the attacks?

... No.

Aunt? Uncle?

I'm at my dad's place.

By yourself?

What is this, a therapy session?

If that's what you need it to be.

At first I thought he was mocking me, then realized he genuinely looked concerned. What did she tell you? I asked.

Where were you when planes hit? he asked quietly.

In school. Second period. They had the TV on.

Any of the other students have parents in the buildings?

Just one, this friend of my girlfriend's at the time. Nothing happened though. Her dad was out of town. After that I'd catch her like, looking at me during class with this guilt that made me sick. I would have rather she just be happy about it, cause I know she must have been. Between her and my girlfriend it was like sympathy overkill. I couldn't take it anymore so I slept with her to get rid of them both... So, that was weird.

What?

How I just told all that to a cop.

All I got is time.

No, all you had was time. Check your love handles.
You're past your prime, buddy.

You do that a lot, don't you? Play the asshole?

I am an asshole, so it's not that difficult.

You ever lay a hand on one of your girlfriends?

The question took me off-guard. He locked eyes with
me, studying my expression. I bowed my head, remembering
those confused moments when I realized what I'd done.
Whatever the consequences, I decided to be honest. Yes.

More than once?

I shook my head, then added, But I've had this temper
as long as I can remember. It takes everything I have to
control it. She's just really good at getting it out of me.

The girl in there?

Yes.

You give her some of those bruises?

Yes.

... But you also defended her?

I tried.

Explain that to me.

I didn't know how to start, so I kept my mouth shut.

Here's the situation. You can either talk here or at the
station, but you're going to talk.

... She tapped into a part of me that I thought was dead.
And then she fucked around with it. I was drunk and lost
control. But when that jerkoff was hurting her, I felt
something totally different. Like it was my job to protect her.
That if I lost her, that part of me was going to seal back up
again.

The officer sighed. His breath showed in the air. After a
moment he said, You got dealt a bum hand, kid. Sooner you
get over that the better. And quit the drinking.

CONCRETE FEVER

The response hit me wrong. It cheapened everything. Is that like, your five minute diagnosis of me?

Just a suggestion.

I got baggage.

I'm sure you do.

I mean it. I'm not all about the attacks. It's not like, my reason for being.

So what is?

How should I know? Did you know you wanted to be an overweight cop when you were my age?

His mustache lifted into a smile. Remember that more often.

Remember what? I asked.

How early in the game you are, and what a waste it'd be to call it quits.

He turned me around and unlocked the handcuffs. I brought my arms back in front of me and rubbed my wrists where the metal had choked down. He handed me my ID. Seeing my picture somehow took me by surprise. I looked like such a poser. Such a would-be punk. I looked back up and asked, So, what now?

Now, someone takes you home, he said.

Just like that?

Just like that.

... What about her?

Her car already left. Not for nothing, but I'd suggest giving it a day before you call. And don't skimp on the apology. Any girl that can tolerate your bullshit is worth holding onto for dear life.

***

The police car sped up the avenues, my driver silent at the wheel. He was a rookie, intensely listening to the static of the police scanner, no doubt cursing his assignment to drive all the way uptown and back. I never saw the pit, I realized out loud.

You don't want to see that, he said.

Have you?

Yeah.

What's it look like?

He looked at me in the rearview. You kidding? After a moment he shifted in his seat and added, It's going to be like the Empire State Building. That platform. Nobody who actually lived here it is actually going to look.

An old couple was exiting my building when we pulled up. The rookie letting me out of the cruiser caught their attention. They looked disappointed but not surprised. Couldn't afford a cab, I said as I walked through. Waiting for the elevator, I heard movement in the first floor apartment. The day was starting. The sidewalks wouldn't be clear for long. If I was going to go through with it I had to be quick.

I got off on the penthouse floor and took the steps to the roof. Halfway up I stopped and turned back. I keyed into my warzone of an apartment and searched for Gypsy's stash. I finally found it by the sink, under her drawing of Papa Smurf getting pissed on by an evil sun. I held my hand under the faucet and traced a finger over the lipstick. I brought under my nose and inhaled its scent. Touched it to my lips. Tasted her lips again. Felt my chest tear open. Resolved, I stopped the water and headed out of the apartment.

On the roof, the day had finally broken. A blanket of clouds covered the sky but the quality of grey proved the sun in the back somewhere. I walked to the shattered possessions of what's-his-name and kicked them into a corner. I stacked the shards in a sort of pyramid with Gypsy's prescription bottles hidden inside. Anyone else would think it was just a bunch of trash, not worth noticing. She'd get the message though. Somehow she had the foresight to leave them behind, keeping us out of jail and giving me the opportunity to finish off the night as intended. The least I could do was make sure she got them back.

I found concrete blocks weighing down a satellite dish. I carried them one-by-one to the ledge overlooking Amsterdam Avenue. The dish was bolted into the rooftop, the weights seemed overkill. I doubted any amount of wind between now and the investigation would disrupt the TV habits of Mr. and Mrs. Such-and-such.

I stepped onto the blocks and eased my way up onto the ledge itself. The wind seemed to whip harder now that I was exposed. The sidewalk was clear of people. The timing was perfect. I counted down from five but stopped at one and a half. I invented a reason to wait. I wanted to see the sun break through the clouds.

My heart skipped at the sound of feet gracefully landing behind me from an adjacent rooftop. She cleared her throat. I resisted looking, but asked, How did you get away?

Gave them your address.

And they let you go?

Big eyes, shiny smile, she said.

Why am I not surprised, I said, staring out. Blood pulsed against my eardrums. Did you ever feel anything for me at all?

Yes, she said.

Don't say yes if you don't mean it.

A few cars passed below. Her silence made me furious.

You were out for blood.

If that's what you think...

I'm jumping when the dawn breaks.

It's already...

The sun. I want to see the sun.

Another thing stopping you, huh?

I'm not kidding.

You wouldn't want to forget this.

I turned to look at her for the first time. In her hand was my father's flask. She placed it on the ledge, then hoisted herself up beside me. She looked out, the bruises hidden on the far side of her profile. Her skin was chalk white, her limbs stretched thin. I imagined her dissolving into the air. Only her eyes were solid. They stared out across the city, settling somewhere out on the horizon. I bent down and picked up the flask. There was a sip left. I opened it up and inhaled. Indentifying the subtle flavors as they came to me, no matter how absurd. Burnt cedar. Wet soil. Smoke. Then I poured it as a libation over the edge. A few seconds later it hit the sidewalk unnoticed. I sensed her watching. Food for fish, I said. Then I spun the cab back in place and set the flask down away from us. It'd be a shame if we jumped off together.

Not for me, she said simply. I'd just fly off into the sunrise.

I clenched a fist and took a step toward her. There wasn't any magic.

Her blank expression slowly lifted into a smile. Don't you remember, Jumper? I'm your guardian angel.

I drew close. Without warning she kissed me. Such love and anger surged through me, I didn't know what to make of it. I took her wrists in one hand and reached for the small of her back with the other. I leaned her over the edge and sheer terror lit across her face. I felt satisfied. There was no magic. She wasn't some angel sent to save me. I knew you wouldn't fly, I said. You'd fall right down with me!

Stop it, Jumper! It can't happen like this! It has to be us together! Pull me up!

She kneed me in the crotch and righted herself on the ledge. The strength left me and I lost my balance. I started to fall. As I saw the roof disappear from under me a sense of relief took hold. Then I felt a tug on the back of my jacket and everything came into focus again. My feet found the ledge again. We each took a step back, panting, staring at one another in absolute quiet.

The sun broke through the clouds.

You should have let me go, I said.

Why? she asked. So you wouldn't have to do it yourself?

There was zero malice in her comment. It was the truth of it that killed me. I steadied myself, then stepped to face out. A thousand painters would've killed for a sunrise like that. In the time since she arrived, the sky had erupted from a dull grey into a chaos of blues and yellows, pinks and reds, oranges, greens, countless shades of purple. Briefly I lost track of everything and thought I was on a mountaintop, receiving some sort of divine revelation.

Gypsy took my hand, pulling me from the fantasy. She made no attempt to guide me from the ledge. Her intentions were crystal clear. Forward or back, we were going together. I allowed myself to get lost in her eyes, and my heart swelled with gratitude for her being there. Squeezing her hand I looked toward the dawn, and at last embraced the relief and terror of what was coming next.

***

For a brief moment I was suspended, then felt a drop. A slow rocking from side to side. The security of cushioning. I lifted a heavy hand and wiped my eyes clean, just in time to catch the last minutes of sunset out the train window. Patched wheat fields blurred together as we whipped past. I focused on one in the distance and searched for a farmhouse. As far as I could see there was none. Just a huge plot of fertile land out there, waiting to be claimed.

I breathed deep, feeling my lungs expand against the soft seatback. Resting my head, I watched thin clouds tangle themselves against a darkening blue sky. No matter how fast we sped, I knew we'd never catch them. They'd always be just ahead of us, teasing.

Gypsy shifted her head on my shoulder. Fast asleep and smiling in her dream. We'd made connections in nondescript towns, the terrain gradually flattening out. I realized with a grin that I'd forgotten the next destination. At some point the tracks would run out and we'd find our place. Somewhere all our own, where we could get a fresh start. The compartment lights dimmed as the sun fell out of sight. My breathing slowed. My limbs felt heavy. I watched the world slowly fade to black.

ACKNOWLEDGEMENTS

The author wishes to acknowledge those who helped him bring this story from stagework to fiction.

The play's original New York production would have been nothing without the efforts of Nell Casey, Michael V. Rudez, Jessie T. Kressen, Sonya Cooke, Dan Waldron, Campbell Ringel, Mattie Cogliano, Stacey Maltin, and Anthony Abdallah. The Drama Book Shop, Michael Roderick, Peter Loffredo, Iris McQuillan-Grace, Adam David Jones, Lara St. Thomas, and Geoff Murphy aided in the script's development. From Jumper's earliest days, Michael Mraz endowed the character with a humanity and hunger that helped shape the author's vision. Accompanying him, Kimberly DiPersia served as inspiration for the book's illustrations.

The novel found its voice among the founding members of the Greenpoint Writers Group: Michael Abramson, Rose Casanova, Laura Deffley, Christianne Hedtke, Crispin Kott, Alex Ivanov, and Kathy Lindboe. Logan Medland, Danielle

Pollack, Chris Tarry, Laura Weinert-Kendt, Jessica Glazer, Mark Souza, and Cydney McQuillan-Grace also contributed feedback during various stages of the book's development.

Word Bookstore in Greenpoint, Brooklyn, served as the unofficial home for this novel, as their enthusiasm and generosity toward local writers allowed the book to find its voice. Jenn Northington, in particular, provided guidance with the book's first edition.

The author also wishes to acknowledge his family for their love and support, especially his grandmother for her years of enthusiasm and guidance on his work.

NATHANIEL KRESSEN is a Brooklyn-based playwright, screenwriter, and novelist. His plays have been published by The Good Ear Review, One Act Play Depot, and YouthPlays; workshopped at PS 122, Soho Rep Walkerspace, and NYU's Tisch School of the Arts; and produced in ten states and counting. His screenplay *Adopting Skins* won first place in The Relevance Group's American Details Competition, and was filmed in the summer of 2011. His short fiction appears in The Battered Suitcase, a quarterly review published by Vagabondage Press. *Concrete Fever* is his first novel.